"Just what is your problem, Emily?" Paris demanded. "You've been giving me dirty looks ever since you sat down to dinner."

Emily's eyes narrowed. "And after you've obviously slaved over a hot stove all day, too."

"So what if I didn't cook dinner?" Paris said, exasperated. "I still arranged for it. I still put it on the table."

"That's not the point," Emily said. "Everyone else cooks when it's his or her turn. You think that just because you have money, you're above that."

"Oh, you are so self-righteous," Paris spat out, throwing down her napkin and pushing back her chair. "I can't stand another minute of this. My head is pounding."

"Paris—" Michael said.

"Oh, spare me whatever soothing thing you're going to say," Paris snapped. "It's your fault I feel so rotten, anyway, after last night."

Emily's eyes widened. She pushed back her chair, too. "I see," she said. She looked from Paris to Michael. "I see exactly how it is now."

Never Fall in Love

Dahlia Kosinski

HarperPaperbacks
A Division of HarperCollinsPublishers

HarperPaperbacks   *A Division of* HarperCollins*Publishers*
                    10 East 53rd Street, New York, N.Y. 10022

Copyright © 1995 by Daniel Weiss Associates, Inc., and Dahlia Kosinski
All rights reserved. No part of this book may be used or reproduced in any manner whatsoever without written permission of the publisher, except in the case of brief quotations embodied in critical articles and reviews. For information address HarperCollins*Publishers*, 10 East 53rd Street, New York, N.Y. 10022

Cover photography by Herman Estevez
Back cover photograph of house by FPG

First printing: November 1995

Printed in the United States of America

HarperPaperbacks and colophon are trademarks of HarperCollins*Publishers*

❖ 10 9 8 7 6 5 4 3 2 1

*With many thanks to Hilary Steinitz,
Liz Craft, and Leslie Morganstein.*

•   •   •

*For Ian, who encouraged me to
stay home in my pajamas.*

Chapter 1

EMILY HESS LEANED FORWARD IN the Oldsmobile, resting her head on the seat back between her brother, Michael, who was driving, and her best friend, Holly Wright. Hanging forward this way made Emily feel six years old instead of eighteen, but she couldn't help it. They were here in Boulder *finally*, ready to start school *finally*, after what had to be the longest, most anticipation-filled summer of anyone's life, anywhere. They were finally here, they were about to see their new house, and Emily couldn't wait.

Her brother Michael glanced at her, the laugh lines around his blue eyes deepening. "Are you going to ask if we're there yet?" he teased. "You've been thumping your foot against the back of my seat for about an hour now."

"I have not!" Emily protested. "I'm just anxious to see our house. Rachel left that message last night . . . it made me kind of nervous."

Michael nodded. "She started to say that there was something not exactly wrong with the house—then she coughed twice and hung up." He grinned. "But it'll be okay. I'm sure of it."

Emily smiled back at Michael. It was good to see him acting happy and excited. Sometimes he seemed so sophisticated and world-weary that Emily felt as though she were decades younger than he was, instead of just ten months. He was wearing tan pants that weren't wrinkled despite hours of driving, and a white shirt that looked as though it had just been ironed. His dark, curly hair, if a little rumpled, still looked good. That was the maddening thing about Michael's hair, at least to Emily—he could walk through a hurricane and his hair would still arrange itself into an artful bunch of waves. Actually, Michael was maddening in many ways—including the fact that he was so handsome he could look good in those boring ultra-conservative clothes he wore.

"Read me the directions, will you?" Michael said to Holly.

Holly jumped a little bit, and then looked guiltily at the scribbled notes in her lap. She had been daydreaming, Emily was fairly sure. Holly daydreamed constantly, and she tended to flinch almost anytime anyone spoke to her. Once she had shown Emily her ninth-grade report card. There was a little box where teachers could write sinister, prophetic codes about you that you had to look up and decode on the back of the report card. For example, if the teacher wrote "J" on the back, you looked it up and it meant "Works conscientiously," which was fine, but if the teacher wrote "K" in the box, that meant "Disrupts class," and your parents got all agitated and thought you were turning into a hoodlum. But anyway, one of Holly's teachers had written a "Q" in the box and—because the decoding list on the back only went up to "P"—the teacher had *handwritten* "Q— Excessive daydreaming."

Now Holly looked at the directions that Michael and Emily's cousin Rachel had sent them. "Turn left on Mapleton," she read in her soft voice. "Oh, wait, we already did that . . . now we're on Eighteenth, so Spruce Street should be right around here. . . . Hey, that girl looks a lot like Rachel."

Michael and Emily burst out laughing because it *was* their cousin Rachel, standing on the sidewalk in front of a dilapidated old green house. Holly blushed, and Emily leaned forward to ruffle her hair.

"Stop dreaming, sweetheart," Emily whispered. She called Holly by a thousand endearments: honeybunch, sugarplum, dollface, chicken little, kitten, kitty, sugar, jam. She never thought twice about it. Holly seemed to require a lot of mothering.

Holly twisted around to look at Emily, a gentle smile on her lips. She was tiny, barely over five feet, with curly caramel-colored hair and large brown eyes that dominated her small, elfin face. Right now her eyes were happy but apprehensive. "Well, we're here," she said softly.

The three of them climbed out of the car and hugged Rachel, who was wearing a Lycra jogging outfit. Her dark hair was pulled into a ponytail.

"Emily! Michael! Holly!" she exclaimed, hugging each one in turn. "Oh, I'm so glad you guys are going to move into this house. You're going to love it."

Emily looked at the green house a little anxiously. Its paint was peeling off in large flakes. "We got your message yesterday on the answering machine," she said. "And you said that you had to tell us something about the house."

"Well, yes," Rachel said, looking distinctly nervous. "Come on inside and look at it."

"Rachel . . . " Michael began, but she was already walking ahead of them across the patchy, overgrown lawn toward a front door that sagged on its hinges.

"Let's start at the top floor," Rachel said. She led them up a wide staircase, which creaked alarmingly. Each stair sloped dramatically in the middle.

If I were a writer, Emily thought, *I would think what a great short story this would be. If I were a carpenter, it would be my dream come true. But I'm just an environmental science major who's worried about breaking her neck on these steps.*

They went up two flights. At the top of the stairs Rachel paused for breath. She pointed to a small, winding wrought-iron staircase. "That leads to the attic," she said. "Then there are two bedrooms on this floor and two on the floor below. Plus a basement."

"Rachel—" Emily began. She wondered how long Rachel would continue talking in this quick, excited way before she told them whatever it was she had to tell them.

4

"So I figured you could each have a bedroom and a study—or a studio in your case, Holly," Rachel said.

"It seems perfect." Holly was an art student. "But your message sounded so . . . ominous. Is there a problem?"

"Well." Rachel bit her lip. "A small one."

Michael narrowed his eyes. "How small?"

Rachel sighed. "The house is condemned."

"*What?*" they chorused, horrified.

Rachel held up her hands. "It's not as bad as it sounds," she said soothingly. "In fact, it may turn out to be to your advantage."

Emily felt like crying. "Rachel, you said this house was all set! I gave up my chance at a dorm room for this!"

"Just hear me out," Rachel said. "The house is condemned because it's so old and considered un—because it's so old."

She was about to say it's considered unsafe, Emily thought, feeling her stomach knot.

"Anyway," Rachel continued, "the owner has to pay to have it torn down and he doesn't want to do that, so he's claiming that he doesn't own it after all. He says that the previous owner never sold it."

Michael sat down heavily on the bottom step of the winding staircase. "Oh, man," he said.

"You're not listening," Rachel said, exasperated. "The owner and the previous owner are going to be in court for *years* straightening this out. Meanwhile, neither one can charge rent because that would indicate ownership. I asked my dad." Rachel's dad was an attorney.

"This is terrible," Emily moaned. She still felt close to tears.

"Wait a minute," Holly said quietly. "We could live here rent-free? All year?"

"Hallelujah!" Rachel said. "One of you is listening, at least."

"We don't pay any rent?" Michael said skeptically. "What happens when the court case is settled?"

"Like I said, that won't be for years," Rachel said confidently. "You'll be gone with the wind by then, trust me."

"I hope so," Michael said wryly.

Emily frowned. "Michael, you're not actually considering . . . ?"

"Why not?"

"Because—because the house is condemned."

"It seems safe enough to me," Michael said. "Rachel lived here all last year and no chunks of plaster fell on her." He glanced at their cousin. "Or did they?"

Rachel shook her head.

"But—" Emily faltered. "What about gas and electricity?"

"Neither the owner nor the previous owner will cut them off," Rachel answered smoothly. "That would also constitute ownership. I checked."

Holly sat down on the step next to Michael and rested her chin in her hand. Her small face looked dreamy. "I could have my own studio," she said. "I'd never be able to afford that anywhere else."

Michael put his arm around her. "That's the attitude." He looked at Emily appealingly. "Come on, Em. This way we wouldn't have to get jobs. Think of all the time you could spend studying. You'll have a four-point-oh average, no problem."

Emily sighed. "This is probably illegal," she said.

Michael didn't blink. Rachel rubbed her toe on the floor.

Holly brushed a wisp of brown hair off her forehead. "Please, Emily," she said. "It'll be fun."

Emily looked at the faces of her brother and best friend. Holly looked hopeful, Michael slightly challenging. *He thinks I won't do it,* she thought. *He thinks I'm too uptight or something.*

Emily shrugged. "Okay," she said. "I can't fight you both."

Holly hopped off the stairs and hugged Emily. "Great!" she said softly.

Emily looked at her friend closely. Holly was glowing with happiness. "Hey, you're really excited about this, aren't you?"

"Well, sure," Holly said. "This way we don't have to share a dorm with a bazillion other girls, *and* I can have a studio, *and* it's our own place, *and* think of all the money we'll save—"

"Okay, okay," Emily said, laughing. "I see your point." She knew that Holly was too shy to enjoy the perpetual slumber-party atmosphere of a dorm. It was one of the reasons Emily had agreed to this house in the first place. Neither she nor Holly was really tailor-made for dorm life, Holly because of shyness, Emily because she was so intense.

Emily turned to Rachel. "How about the rest of the tour?"

Rachel looked relieved. She showed them the two bedrooms on the third floor. One was a perfect square, with a large dormer window placed exactly in the middle of one wall.

"Oh, this is perfect," Holly exclaimed.

Michael and Emily exchanged an amused glance. Holly was so visually oriented. "Then this will be your room, buttercup," Emily said. Her spirits were rising. "And I'll have the bedroom next door, if that's okay with you," she said to Michael.

He smiled. "Sure. I'll take a bedroom on the second floor so I don't have to share a bathroom with the two of you."

They could barely wrench Holly out of her new room to explore the rest of the house. Emily's room was larger, with an ancient walk-in closet. The attic was long and narrow, but fairly sunny. Its floor sloped slightly.

"That must be why the place is condemned," Michael said.

On the second floor there were two large bedrooms. Michael chose the one with more windows. On the main floor was a kitchen, a tiny dining room, and a living room complete with sagging, threadbare couches. They checked out the basement, which was huge, cavernous, and paneled.

Holly wrinkled her nose at the paneling. "Somebody must've put that up hoping to brighten this place," she said critically. "It didn't work."

Emily laughed.

Rachel sighed. "I know what you mean, Holly,"

she said. "This was my room. In fact, I still have to get some clothes out of the closet."

"We should bring our own stuff in," Michael said. "The moving guys are going to be here with the bedroom furniture in a little while."

They left Rachel in the basement and filed back up the stairs, out of the house, and onto the lawn, where Michael stopped so abruptly that Emily ran into him.

"Hey, what's the deal?" she asked. Then her eyes widened.

A suntanned guy was standing on the sidewalk. He had chin-length blunt-cut hair bleached blond by the sun, with small, darker sideburns. His face was broad and even-featured, with mild hazel eyes and very white teeth.

He had a huge backpacking-around-Europe-sized backpack on his shoulders. Scattered across the lawn were four pairs of skis and boots, three snowboards, two pairs of ski poles, two duffel bags, a laundry bag (full), a couple of ski jackets, one pair of ski pants, three pairs of running shoes, a tennis racquet, a squash racquet, numerous loose tennis balls, and a bunch of bungee cords. He was wearing Rollerblades.

The suntanned boy smiled. "Hey," he said. "Are you guys going to be living here, too?"

He was easily the most handsome boy Emily had ever seen.

Oh, no, Holly thought as soon as she saw the blond guy and his eight million possessions. *He's*

*going to move in here, and everything will be all
awkward and strange.*

Holly didn't like things to change. When she
was small, she had once cried for two days
straight when her mother repapered her bedroom. She was too timid to enjoy meeting people—especially people as bold and brash-looking
as this blond guy—and she was too quiet for most
people to seek her out. Holly always felt as though
life was passing her by, and she didn't particularly
blame life for doing so. There was nothing exciting
about Holly Wright, she thought. She wasn't like
Emily, who fairly vibrated with brilliance and
intensity. She wasn't like Michael, who oozed
sophistication.

(This was something Holly's mother had said
about Michael. "That boy's too slick," she said.
"He reminds me of a boy I knew in college. My
roommate used to say, 'Oozing charm from every
pore, he oiled his way across the floor.'" Holly
didn't think this was a very nice thing to say about
somebody, and she especially didn't think it was a
very nice thing for her *mother* to say about somebody, but she had to admit that it was kind of
accurate.)

But, at any rate, she loved Emily, brilliant or
not, and she was *used* to Michael, slick or not. She
didn't want this blond stranger with the bright
white smile weaseling in.

So Holly was vastly relieved when Michael said
to the stranger, "I'm sorry, but the house is
already rented." Michael would take care of this.
His slickness was good for that.

But the blond guy frowned. "Rented? How can this house be rented? It's condemned."

"Well, yes," Michael admitted. "I guess I should have said that it's taken."

"By the three of you?" The blond guy raised an eyebrow.

They nodded. "I'm sorry," Holly said.

"So the three of you are going to rattle around in this big house by yourselves?" the blond guy said. He frowned again. Holly was beginning to feel uncomfortable.

"Well," Michael began. He seemed unsure of how to continue, which was not something Holly had seen in him before. "Well," he said again, "it's just that we were already *planning* to move in, and—"

"Well, I've been planning to move in since yesterday, when I heard the house was condemned and rent-free," the blond guy said. His voice was very mild. There was only the slight frown to suggest—to suggest—

He's making us feel selfish, Holly thought with surprise. *He's doing a good job, too.*

The blond guy cleared his throat softly. "Look," he began.

His voice is just oh-so-reasonable, Holly thought with mounting horror. *Whatever he says, he's going to be right, I just know it.*

"I know you probably weren't planning on an extra housemate, but it's a huge house, and now it's a free house, and—"

Emily's blue eyes flashed. "Listen, we just told you that the house is taken," she said. "I don't

care how big or how free it is, it's *ours*. Now I'm
very sorry for any inconvenience this may have
caused you, but really—"

The blond guy's white teeth were showing in
his tanned face. "I see," he said. "I assume you
have a lease proving that the house belongs to
you?"

Emily opened her mouth and then shut it with a
snap. She began fiddling with the ends of her
black hair. Michael was very carefully studying
the ground. Only Holly met the boy's eyes.

Holly thought the blond guy was awfully nice
not to get angry with three people who were trying to edge him out of a house he wanted to move
into. If she were him, she probably would have
burst into tears and fled down the street.

The blond guy held her gaze for a moment.
Then he grinned and threw her one of his duffel
bags. "Help me with this, won't you?" he said.

And Holly, who was shy to the point of hesitat-
ing before ordering a pizza, grinned back.

The beautiful blond boy's name was Mac Niles. He
introduced himself with a smile, shaking hands all
around. Emily held out her hand casually. *Okay,*
she thought. *This guy is fodder for my fantasy life
for the next ten years and he happens to be moving
in, but no big deal. Right?*

Mac held her hand briefly. "Emily," he said, his
eyes flicking over her.

Then he turned and shook hands with Holly,
smiling gently. "Hello, Holly," he said pleasantly.

Why, he understands, Emily thought with surprise. *He understands how we treat Holly. How can he know that after just meeting us?*

Next Mac gathered up nearly half the equipment spread over the lawn. He stalked across the yard in his Rollerblades, doing a strange sort of duck waddle. Holly trailed along behind him with his duffel bag in her arms. Rachel ran ahead to open the door.

Michael and Emily looked at each other and shrugged. They each picked up a pair of skis from the remaining stuff.

"I have to say," Emily said quietly, "this isn't exactly what I'd pictured."

"Which part?" Michael laughed. "The condemned house? The surfer housemate?"

Emily smiled faintly. "All of it, I guess," she said. She hefted Mac's skis high in her arms. "Michael, do you really think it's going to be okay? We're living in this house without paying rent . . . what if we get thrown out?"

Michael squeezed her shoulder. "If we have to move in a few months, then we'll have to move," he said reassuringly. "But we'll still be ahead because we'll have saved money."

"But what will Mom and Dad think?"

"Mom and Dad never have to know," Michael said firmly. "At least, I hope not. . . . Emily, it's going to be great. That Mac guy seems nice, and it's a huge house." His face broke into a smile, not his lopsided cynical smile, but a truly happy one. "Everything will be okay. I promise."

Emily smiled back at him. She wondered about

people without older brothers, wondered where they found comfort and how they clung to the illusion that everything would be okay.

The noise of a loud motor interrupted her thoughts. They looked down the street to see a VW van painted in camouflage colors pull up to the curb. The van gave a final coughing wheeze and mercifully fell silent.

A skinny bare-chested boy wearing jeans and a red bandanna wrapped around his head jumped out of the driver's-side door. He had a light brown goatee and flashing green eyes. "Hi!" he said to them. "Are you my new housemates?" His eyes moved over them and lingered on Emily. He smiled wryly. "Well, well, well. There is a God."

Chapter 2

HOLLY WATCHED MAC DUMP HIS huge armful of stuff onto the floor of the bedroom next to Michael's.

"Whew," he said, rubbing his arms. He grinned at her. "Ready for another trip?"

"Sure," she said softly. She liked Mac already— he kept conversation flowing so smoothly and didn't seem to require anything from her. Holly hated it when people asked her questions that called for complex or witty answers. For example: *Are you looking forward to art school? Why don't you like to go swimming? What were you thinking when you bought those pants?*

In speech class in high school, the teacher had gone on and on about how truly good conversationalists asked open-ended questions, and how this enabled the other person to natter on about himself and feel really important. Well, Holly hated open-ended questions. She liked nice, simple closed-ended ones, such as the ones Mac asked. *Ready for another trip? Mind if I take this room? Isn't it great that we don't have to pay rent?* With Mac, she could just answer "yes" or "no" or "sure" or "I think so," and she didn't have to try to whip up a witty monologue on the spot.

She trailed along after Mac as he bounded down the stairs. Halfway down they met Emily and Michael coming up. With them was a skinny boy whose eyes sparkled with mischief.

"This is our other new housemate, Dane Caroll," Emily said shortly. She sounded angry. Holly wondered if she had already clashed with the new boy. She looked at Dane. He didn't seem offensive to her—just hyper. Excitable. A lot like Emily, come to think of it.

Behind them were four other guys, each balancing an amplifier the size of a small refrigerator.

"Hello," Mac said easily. "Are you all moving in?"

"No, just me," the boy named Dane said. He stepped forward and shook hands with Mac and Holly.

Holly nodded and then said timidly, "Aren't your friends getting tired?"

"Hey, shoot, you're right," Dane said, glancing at his friends. "Sorry, guys." He turned to Emily. "Where did you say the spare room was?"

Emily pushed her bangs off her forehead. "I thought the room next to Michael's," she began, then looked at Mac and Holly. "Unless . . . "

"I just put my stuff in there, but I can move," Mac said.

"Well, there's the basement and the attic," Emily said. She looked prettily flustered, and Holly saw Dane studying her closely. *He'll be in love with her in an hour,* she thought. Well, that was nothing new.

"No problem," Dane said. "I'll take the basement. I sleep a lot during the day anyway. Come on, guys. Emily, will you show us the way?"

Emily's eyebrows drew together in annoyance, but she led the group of boys off down the hall. The arms of the four boys were quivering. Dane was at her side, not carrying a thing.

Mac, Michael, and Holly went back into the front yard. Mac's trail of possessions looked less imposing, but a cornucopia of speakers, guitars, loose wires, magazines, and T-shirts spilled out of the VW van.

Whistling, Mac gathered up another load of his ski equipment.

Holly caught Michael's arm as Mac went back into the house. "What's the story with Dane?" she asked quietly.

"He's in a band, as you can see," Michael explained with a sigh. "It was like with Mac—they knew about the house, and technically we do have the room. It's not like we're paying rent, either."

"I know," Holly said. "It's just that I thought it was going to be the three of us, and I'd barely gotten used to it being the *four* of us, and now . . . "

"I know exactly what you mean," Michael said. He smiled a little bit. "But now the house is full, right?"

"It's full?" said a crestfallen voice from behind them.

Holly turned to see a girl with long blond hair

standing on the sidewalk. She was wearing a short plaid skirt and knee socks and a turtleneck sweater with a dark blue blazer. She looked like a Catholic-school girl.

No, Holly corrected herself, *she looks like a model pretending to be a Catholic-school girl.* Suddenly Holly felt dusty and rumpled in her shorts and T-shirt.

"Hello," Michael said to the girl.

"Did you just say the house was full?" the girl asked, ignoring his greeting. "I was hoping—well, I heard it was rent-free, and I thought . . ." Her large blue eyes shifted from Michael to Holly and back.

"Hello, Paris," Rachel said from the porch. She had about a dozen shirts slung over her arm. "You heard about the house, too?"

"Well, sure," the girl said. "Are all the rooms really taken? I heard there were six."

"There isn't—" Michael began.

"Why do you want to live here, anyway?" Rachel broke in. "You can afford to live anywhere."

Paris tucked a strand of hair behind her ear. "Just because I can afford to pay rent doesn't mean I enjoy it," she said. "I'd rather spend my money on other things."

Emily came out onto the porch behind Rachel. She saw Paris, and an expression Holly couldn't quite read flickered across her face. "Hi," she said cautiously.

Paris smiled. "Hi."

"Emily, this is Paris Newman. Paris, this is my cousin, Emily Hess," Rachel said tonelessly.

"Nice to meet you," Paris said. She smiled again. Her teeth were tiny and even and pearly.

"Paris wants to move into the attic," Michael said.

Holly stared at Michael, open-mouthed. Hadn't he just said that she could stop worrying, that all the rooms were full?

Paris looked at him gratefully. "Oh, so there's still a space?" she said. "I'm so happy, I—"

"Paris," Rachel interrupted, "come off it. Your father makes more money than anyone in Colorado, practically. You don't need to live rent-free. Why not leave the room for someone else?"

Paris narrowed her eyes. "I would appreciate it if you didn't broadcast what you may or may not know about my financial background," she said coolly. Rachel flushed. "Besides, the place isn't being turned into a homeless shelter, is it? I mean, you all"—she gestured to Michael and Holly—"weren't chosen on the basis of *need,* were you?"

Michael laughed suddenly, breaking the tension. "She's right, Rachel," he said. "We've been operating on a first-come-first-served basis. No reason to stop now."

Emily frowned slightly. "Michael, I think we should at least run it by Mac and Dane."

"Run what by Mac and Dane?" Dane asked, sauntering onto the porch with Mac.

"This is Paris," Michael said. "She wants to move into the attic."

"Oh," Mac said, sounding disappointed. "I just went up there and *I* wanted to move into the attic.

The floor slopes, and I thought I could practice my Rollerblading."

"Even better," Michael said. "Paris can have the room next to mine, then."

"Michael—" Emily began.

"Sounds cool," Dane said. "Good to meet you, Paris." He walked across the yard and began rummaging around in his van.

Holly wished she could be as nonchalant as Dane. It wasn't that she didn't like Paris; it was just that poised, well-put-together people made her nervous. Except for Emily, of course. And Paris was so picture-perfect that she made even Emily seem not as flawless-looking as usual.

"I'll go move my stuff up to the attic," Mac said, and went back inside.

"So it's all set," Michael said. He and Paris smiled at each other in the bright fall sunshine.

Holly met Emily's eyes and shrugged.

As soon as Michael took Paris into the house, Holly joined Emily and Rachel on the porch. Rachel was getting ready to leave.

"Sorry about this," Rachel said. "I really thought this was going to be the perfect deal for you."

"You don't like Paris, do you?" Emily asked bluntly.

Rachel shook her head. "I barely know her," she said. "But she has a reputation for being very . . . callous. And she's wealthy and tends to flaunt it. I just don't trust her."

"Neither do I," Emily said.

Holly looked at her friend. "You only met her for a nanosecond, Em."

"I know." Emily sighed. "But there was something about the way she was standing there, looking so forlorn in her—her little—"

"Her Catholic-school outfit," Holly finished.

Emily laughed. "So you don't like her, either."

"I didn't say that," Holly protested. "But I do know what you mean about the outfit. She seems like an actress playing a part. Like all of a sudden she's going to stand up and announce that we've all been unwittingly participating in a psych experiment."

This had, in fact, once happened to Holly in a shopping mall. She had gone into the ladies' room and when she came out of the stall, there were all these men milling around who told her that she was in the men's room. Holly checked the sign on her way out and it still said "Ladies." A man caught up to her in the parking lot and said that he was a college professor, that they had been conducting a psych experiment, and that they had hoped Holly would argue with the men in the bathroom and say, "No, no, *you're* in the wrong place, not me. See the sign?" He spent a long time questioning her about her self-esteem. It ranked among the worst days of Holly's life.

"Look, I have to go," Rachel said, checking her watch. "I'm sorry to be leaving town just as you get here, but my oh-so-exciting student-teaching job starts in a couple of days, and I've got a *lot* of driving to do before I get to Birmingham." She smiled. "I hope everything works out." She hugged them each.

Holly and Emily watched her walk to her car and get in. She honked the horn briefly as she drove away.

Then they turned and entered their new home.

Holly thought that if somebody photographed the six of them as they were now, and titled the photograph "House Meeting," anyone who saw it would immediately know exactly what was going on.

They sat in pairs on the ratty, threadbare couches in the living room: Emily and Mac, Dane and Michael, Holly and Paris. These seemed to be neutral pairings, with no special bonds or ulterior motives, which was good.

Emily surveyed everyone's half-expectant, half-jaded faces and hoped this meeting would be painless. She thought it would be, because if there was one thing you learned in high school, it was how to sit around and fake eye contact and cough up the answers you thought other people wanted to hear.

Michael was hoping that Emily wasn't going to suggest a lot of environmentally sound commune-type ideas that he would have to back her up on, being her brother.

Paris was surreptitiously cleaning her fingernails with a pen cap and thinking that this was even more boring—if that was possible—than those stupid getting-to-know-each-other games they used to play at camp.

Dane was admiring the way that Emily's dark

hair fell in thick waves to her shoulders and how her black eyelashes brushed her cheeks. He had never seen a girl look so pretty in a poncho. He hoped the meeting would go on forever so he could keep looking at her.

Mac was reliving, play-by-play, a squash game he'd won five years earlier. He'd once read an account of a POW who said he'd survived the cruelty of prison camp by replaying golf games in his mind. Ever since then, Mac tried to re-create his top ten greatest squash triumphs whenever he thought he was in for something really boring.

Emily sat forward. "Shall we start?" she said.

The meeting lasted a record-breaking two hours and was *so* tedious that Mac relived four entire squash games and only came alive to make two comments.

The first comment was, "I'll second that."

He said this after Emily had tentatively said that she thought there should be no intrahouse dating, and Holly had tentatively agreed.

Michael, Paris, and Dane all turned to look at him, somewhat startled since he had been silent while they had hashed out issues such as respecting one another's privacy, went over questions such as was borrowing something without asking really the same as stealing, and so on and so on.

"You agree?" Paris asked.

"Sure," Mac said.

"Why?"

Mac frowned. Why was she questioning him?

She hadn't questioned Holly or Emily. He stared back at her until she looked away uncomfortably.

(Staring at someone expressionlessly was a trick he'd learned from his father, who was a trial lawyer. Another was never to raise his voice—a quiet voice flusters people more than an angry one. Still another piece of advice his father had given him was never to get a tattoo, because tattoos are what give away eighty-five percent of people trying to live under false names. "Thanks, Dad," Mac had said. "It's nice to know you assume I'm going to live on the run." That had been funny once. Not so much anymore.)

"Well, anyway, that's three of us," Emily said, casting Mac a grateful look. "I just think it would simplify things if we didn't date each other."

Paris ran her fingers through her hair. "Why put limits on anything?" she asked. "I'm starting to feel like—"

"Oh, let's just agree to it, okay?" said Dane, who had seen the appreciative look Emily gave Mac. "I don't think anyone here is going to be the sexual inspiration to the world anyway."

Paris rolled her eyes. "All *right*," she said with a huff.

"Fine by me," Michael said mildly.

"Okay, so we're agreed?" Emily asked.

"Yes, but this includes you and Michael, too," Dane said.

"*We're brother and sister.*"

"It was a joke, Emily," Dane said. "Joke? Ha ha?"

The other time Mac commented was when Emily proposed that since there were six of them,

24

they should each cook dinner for the others one night per week, and everyone fend for him- or herself on Saturday night.

Mac was so charmed by the homespun simplicity of this that he immediately said, "That would be great!"

Everyone turned to look at him.

"You think so?" Dane asked doubtfully.

"Oh, I think it would be nice," Holly said softly.

"Me too," Michael said indifferently. (This was just the type of weirdo communal thing he'd been dreading.)

"Why not?" Paris said, and so it was settled.

Then followed an excruciatingly long segment in which they tried unsuccessfully to hash out about a million housemate dos and don'ts. Finally it was Michael, of all people, who suggested that they each anonymously write down one do or don't on a slip of paper; he would type them up and put them on the refrigerator, and they would become the house rules. It did not occur to Michael that he was suggesting something pretty communelike himself.

So they all got paper, and Michael ran out to the car and brought in his portable typewriter. There was a lot of nervous eraser-nibbling and trying to peer at each other's slips of paper, but finally everyone wrote something down and gave it to Michael, who typed up the rules. They were not especially good rules, because everyone was too concerned with specifics and nobody wanted to waste their rule on something basic like making sure to wash the ring out of the bathtub, but they were rules nonetheless. They read as follows:

Dahlia Kosinski

HOUSE RULES FOR 28 SPRUCE STREET

1. Please *don't* leave fingernail or toenail clippings around.
2. If a boy calls, please *do* make sure to note whether he says to say that he called or whether he wants to be called back. There's a difference!
3. Please *don't* surf endlessly through the TV channels and then complain that there's nothing on.
4. Please *do* refill the ice cube trays when there is more than one but less than three ice cubes left.
5. Please *don't* sing out loud if you can't carry a tune.
6. Please *do* always wash between the tines of every fork.

Chapter 3

THE MOVERS ARRIVED ALL AT
once. The truck carrying Michael's, Emily's, and
Holly's furniture fought for space with the sedan
bearing Paris's five trunks. Meanwhile, Dane's
bandmates had made another deafening trip in
the camouflage van and were carting various
pieces of Salvation Army furniture into the basement. Mac had escaped to the attic and spread
out his sleeping bag. He had no furniture.

Darkness had fallen, and a chill was touching
the September air by the time the various movers
had dropped boxes of fragile items, misplaced
suitcases, tracked mud all over, then been tipped
and sent on their way.

Emily and Holly were hot, sweaty, bruised by
box corners, grouchy from being snapped at by
movers, and covered with cobwebs and dirt and
leaves.

Emily dropped into an armchair that had been
left near the front door. "Oh, man, I have never
been this tired in my entire life," she said. "I can't

even bear to think of all those boxes in my room, waiting to be unpacked."

"I know," Holly said, sitting on the arm of the chair. "Plus I can't remember where I packed the sheets and stuff. It's going to be three A.M. before I get to sleep."

Mac wandered out of the kitchen. He took one look at their dust-smudged faces and smiled sympathetically. "I'm making tea," he said. "Anyone want some?"

"That would be wonderful," Emily said. She sat forward and began picking dust bunnies out of her hair. "How did we get so dirty moving boxes and furniture that I know were perfectly clean two days ago?"

Holly brushed a smear of sawdust from her friend's shoulder. "I guess those moving vans have lots of dust in them," she said.

"Here we go," Mac said, handing them each a steaming mug.

Emily gave him a slow, grateful smile, and Holly saw him hesitate, as though momentarily stunned. Then he gently disentangled a leaf from Emily's hair. "Let me get this for you," he said softly.

Oh, no, him too, Holly thought. It obviously didn't matter to him that Emily's black hair had lost its gloss under a coating of dust, or that her blue eyes were tired and red-rimmed. One smile, directed just at him, and he was gone. Holly wondered if she should get up and excuse herself.

But it was Emily who broke the spell. "Thanks for the tea," she said, rising. "But I'd better start unpacking."

"Speaking of which," Mac said, "on my way down I noticed that both of your beds and mattresses were out in the hall. Didn't the movers set them up?"

"Oh, no!" Holly and Emily said together. They looked at each other.

"I never bothered to check," Holly said sheepishly.

"I just assumed . . ." Emily broke off and groaned. "Well, come on, sweet pea, we have even more to do than we thought."

"Oh, I'd be glad to help you," Mac said. He rose swiftly.

"Thank you," Holly said, standing up.

"But it's not necessary," Emily said hastily. "We'll call you or Michael if we can't manage."

"It's no trouble," Mac said.

"I know," Emily said. She clamped a hand on Holly's arm. "It won't be any trouble for us, either." She began leading Holly toward the stairs.

Holly glanced over her shoulder. Mac looked a little forlorn, standing there in the half-light of the kitchen. She wanted to tell him that he could set up her bed, but she knew already that she wasn't the one he wanted to hear from.

"There. That wasn't so bad," Emily said after she'd helped Holly heave her mattress onto her box spring. They had already set up Emily's bed.

With a groan, Holly dropped onto her bare mattress. "Look," she said exhaustedly, "I'm perfectly willing to get a hernia in order to help you uphold

29

your principles, but I'd like to know what those principles are."

Emily smiled wryly. If only Holly could be so confident and sarcastic around everybody. "You don't have a hernia," she said evasively.

"I do now," Holly said. "Plus I think my spine contracted and I lost an inch of height when we moved the first box spring."

"Well, I'll rub your back," Emily said with a grin.

"Em, come on, why wouldn't you let Mac help us? He could've moved the beds in four seconds. Did you see how much stuff he carried up the stairs earlier? It was amazing."

Emily bit her lip. She didn't want to be having this discussion right now. "Holly, that's sexist," she said haltingly. "We don't need to rely on men for every little thing that requires some physical exertion."

Holly rolled her eyes. "Well, you didn't think it was sexist to let our *movers* make seven thousand trips up two flights of stairs," she pointed out. "Besides, I'm five foot one, and Mac's got to be six foot three or four. That's not sexism, that's basic physics."

"Physics?"

"Yeah. Mass plus volume equals work, or whatever."

Emily started laughing. "You sound like my dad." Emily's father related to everything in complex scientific ways. As a consequence, he overcomplicated everything. It would take him two hours to replace a light bulb, he was so busy thinking about theoretical atoms and virtual reality.

Holly laughed, too. "But really, Emily . . . what would have been the harm in letting Mac help?"

Emily sighed. "I don't know. . . . It's hard to explain."

Holly shrugged and stood up. "Let me show you something."

"What?"

"Come over here." Holly pulled Emily over to the window, opened it, and pointed.

The roof flattened into a tiny terrace between her window and Emily's. On the terrace, some previous tenant had placed a child-sized wrought-iron bench.

Emily smiled. Finally, something about their house that was quaint and lovely, instead of dusty and hazardous. "That's perfect," she said. "Let's sit there for a while right now."

"I thought you'd like it," Holly said.

They climbed out the window carefully and sat on the bench. The night was dark and cool. They could see the lights of Boulder twinkling and the giant shadows of the Rockies in the distance.

After a moment of quiet, Emily resumed the conversation they'd been having earlier as though there had been no interruption. "The thing about Mac is that I don't want to give him any encouragement, in case he likes me."

"In *case?*" Holly said. "He picked a leaf out of your hair, for heaven's sake. I was sitting there with enough leaves and twigs and stuff stuck in my hair to build a fair-sized bird's nest, and he didn't say one word to me."

"Well, so you know what I mean," Emily said.

"What are you worried about? I mean, you're protected by the infamous no-dating rule," Holly reminded her. "Or do you think Mac's not a man of his word? Do you think his passion will override his better intentions and—"

"Oh, please," Emily cut in, a small smile playing at the corners of her mouth. "I just think it would be easier not to get started, is all." *Plus he's way too handsome for his own good,* she thought. *Or for my own good.*

"I like Mac," Holly said stubbornly.

"Oh, I like him, too," Emily said impatiently. "But he's such a jock—"

"He's not!"

"He is, Holly," Emily said. "He doesn't even go to school. He just works downtown in some sporting-goods shop."

"Yeah, but he used to go to some prestigious school back East. I forget the name of it. . . ." Holly frowned, concentrating. "Excalibur? Xavier?"

"Exeter?" said Emily, who knew the way Holly's mind worked.

"That's it!" Holly said triumphantly. "Exeter."

"Are you sure?" Emily said. "Because that's a very exclusive prep school."

"I just said it was prestigious."

Emily looked at Holly suspiciously. "How did you find this out?" she asked.

"He said so."

Emily sighed. She supposed Holly found out a lot of things just by being so quiet. People rushed in to fill up the silence. "Well, so why isn't he at

Harvard or Yale?" she said. "For that matter, why isn't he at school period?"

Holly rolled her eyes. "I don't know," she said. "Why don't you ask *him?* All I'm saying is that I don't think he's a dumb jock."

"I didn't say he was dumb, I just said he was a jock," Emily clarified. "Even if he were a Rhodes scholar, I still wouldn't want to date him. Besides—" She paused.

"Besides what?"

Emily took a deep breath. "Well, I just don't want college to be a big repeat of high school, you know?"

"Oh," Holly said simply. "You mean Frank."

Emily sighed. "Yes, I mean Frank."

Frank had been Emily's boyfriend since the eighth grade. There was nothing wrong with Frank. That was the whole problem. He was the most perfect person Emily knew. He was good-looking, charming, intelligent, athletic, devoted. Yet sometimes after he dropped Emily off at her house on Saturday night, she'd felt like running across the yard, whooping with happiness: *I'm free! I'm free! I don't have to see him again until Monday!* But of course that was silly. She never *had* to see him at all. She could have broken up with him anytime.

But relationships, like all things, get to be a habit. And Frank was so *easy* to have as a boyfriend. Her parents loved him. A lot of other girls loved him. And Frank—Frank loved Emily. She had tried to break up with him three times, and each time he'd worn her down with his tireless affection and patience: *Sure, Emily, if that's what you want, but just think about it for a day or two. Please? Can't you do that for me?*

Luckily, smart Frank got a scholarship to Michigan, and his parents had shipped him off to Ann Arbor. Otherwise, Emily thought with terror, *Frank* would probably be living in the attic of this very house, saying, *Listen, Em, I'm not crowding you, but as far as I'm concerned, we're together forever and—*

"Emily!" Holly cried. "Snap out of it!"

Emily blinked. "What?"

Holly squeezed her arm. "Take it easy," she said. "I'm sorry I mentioned Frank. You turned white as a ghost."

Emily smiled. "It's okay," she said. "You're right. Frank is a big, huge part of high school that I don't want to repeat. That's why I don't want to go out with Mac. I want to meet new people. I don't want to spend the next four years with the very first people I bump into."

Holly's face fell. "Oh. Well, of course you don't."

"Except for you and Michael, of course," Emily added quickly.

"Listen, Emily, I don't want you to feel like I'm holding you back," Holly said firmly. "I mean, I— well, I want to meet new people, too."

Emily touched Holly's arm. "That's not what I meant," she said softly. "I still want to spend as much time with you as possible."

Holly shifted impatiently. "Yeah, I know. I wasn't fishing for compliments. I just hope that moving into this house was the right thing for you."

Without a word, Emily gazed out at the mountains in the distance. How could she ever explain that she felt responsible both for Holly and for Michael? If Emily lived in a dorm, who would introduce Holly to people who might otherwise overlook her? Who would make sure Michael didn't become so polished and cosmopolitan that he forgot he liked to slide pieces of macaroni onto the tines of a fork with his fingers and eat them four at a time? Who would keep Holly's face from getting that scared, pinched look when a hardware-store clerk was rude to her? Who would stop Michael from— Oh, there were so many things, so many ways Emily felt she had to look out for both of them.

She sighed. "I'm going to take a shower," she said to Holly. "I'm sure we both have this bench's diamond pattern marked on the back of our legs."

Michael unpacked quickly. The movers had managed to assemble *his* bed, and had even correctly placed his desk and dresser, so he only had to unpack a few cartons and suitcases.

He hung several pairs of nearly identical khaki pants in the closet, stacked a lot of starched shirts (some still in the wrappers) on the shelves, folded a few sweaters, took a bunch of blazers out of garment bags, hung some ties on his tie rack, unpacked some underwear, rolled all his argyle socks into pairs, and he was set.

He made the bed (with hospital corners) and sat on the edge of it, wondering what to do next.

There was a knock at his door. Paris stuck her head in. "Michael?"

He smiled. "You called?"

She leaned against the doorjamb. "Busy?"

"No, I just finished unpacking. How about you?"

"Yeah, I'm all finished, too. . . ." She wandered around, running a finger along the edge of his dresser absently. She glanced into his closet. "Gosh, you're so *neat.*"

He smiled wryly. "One could say the same thing about you."

She raised an eyebrow. "What do you mean?"

"Well, you just unpacked five trunks, and there's not a hair out of place."

Paris smiled. "I've moved a lot. You get used to it." She sat down next to him on the bed. *Right* next to him. Her leg just barely touched his, and he could smell her shampoo. "Thanks for backing me up today," she said softly.

"Well, I'm not sure I really did anything." Michael shrugged. "We still had an extra room, and there you were."

Paris shifted slightly. The ends of her straight honey-colored hair brushed his arm. "Well, anyway, thank you."

Michael cleared his throat. "So, I guess you're a sophomore?" he asked.

She nodded. "And you're just a freshman, which means I can boss you around."

He grinned. "Is that how it works?"

Paris pushed her hair behind her ear. "What are you studying?" she asked, ignoring his question.

"Premed."

Paris whistled. "That's impressive."

Michael laughed. "Wait and see how I do before you get impressed," he said, although privately he wasn't worried. He always got wonderful grades. "What's your major?"

Paris shrugged and half-smiled. She had a beautiful smile, Michael thought. Her lips were very full and expressive. "I haven't chosen a major yet," she said lightly. "It's something I want to put off for as long as humanly possible." She pulled her legs under her. She was still wearing the short plaid skirt and turtleneck. She looked very young. "So, can we gossip about everybody in the house?" she asked.

Michael smiled. "I don't know—can we? Are you asking my permission?"

"Well, some people hate to gossip," Paris replied. "Some people disapprove. I'm just sounding you out."

"Oh, I like to gossip," said Michael, who had no particular feelings about it one way or another. "I *encourage* it in others."

"Okay," said Paris. "Who should we start with?"

Michael considered. "Well, Emily's my sister, so you can ask me anything about her. I know Holly pretty well, too."

"Holly?" Paris raised her eyebrows. "She's beautiful."

"You think so?" Michael had never given much thought to Holly's looks—she was just Holly. Paris was more his idea of beautiful.

"Absolutely," said Paris. "Those big brown eyes . . . You know something? I think both Mac and Dane have crushes on your sister."

"Really? What makes you think that?"

Paris looked thoughtful. "You can see it in the way they look at her. I mean, even if she says the most boring, trivial thing, they both look totally rapt." She darted a quick glance at him. "Not that she says many trivial or boring things."

Michael laughed. "Sorry about the house meeting," he said. "Emily's just—well, she's very idealistic."

"I can tell," Paris said. She said nothing for a moment, just studied him with her cool blue eyes.

Michael cleared his throat again. He was doing a lot of throat-clearing that night.

"Well, good night," Paris said, standing up. It seemed to Michael that he could feel a gentle breeze touching his arm and leg where a moment earlier he had felt the tingle of contact with Paris.

"Good night," he said.

After she was gone, he tried to recall something she'd said and found that he could only remember how many times she'd touched his arm: five.

He shook his head and stood up, laughing softly to himself.

Emily took a long, hot shower in the bathroom she shared with Holly and Mac, then wrapped herself in her ankle-length white robe. As she braided her damp hair she glanced around the bathroom and smiled to herself. Lipsticks, mascaras, lotions, and brushes were scattered everywhere, and they'd been living in the house for barely ten hours. Mac would probably go crazy.

She went back to her room, unpacked a little until she found some sheets, and then made up her bed. She was eyeing the boxes stacked in the corner, wondering if she should just call it a night, when there was a soft knock at her door.

"Come in," she called, still surveying the boxes.

Dane peered around the edge of her door. "You still awake?" he whispered.

Emily blinked. "Well, I'm standing up and talking to you," she said.

"Oh, good." He came in and sat on the edge of her bed. He looked around. "Hey, this room is really nice. You should see the basement. All that paneling . . . did you have a rec room in your house when you were little?"

"Yes," Emily said, not sure why he wanted to talk to her about rec rooms.

"Yeah, well, with all that paneling, I feel like I'm *living* in somebody's rec room." He leaned back on his elbows, stretching out his legs. "And that green carpeting doesn't help. I feel as if there should be a wet bar in the corner and somebody's mom is going to call down the stairs and tell me that dinner's ready."

For a horrible moment Emily was sure that Dane was going to nestle down in her bed and continue talking like that for hours. "Dane," she said abruptly, "can I help you with something?"

He smiled. "I was just wondering if you wanted to walk up to campus with me tomorrow. It's the first day of classes, you know?"

Emily smiled faintly. "Yes, I was aware of that. I didn't know you took classes, though. I thought you were in a band."

Dane laughed. "You sound like my mom," he said. "She always whispers it, like it's this big, shameful secret or something. 'Dane's in—well, in a *band*,' she whispers. Like, 'Dane's in prison.'"

Emily blushed and then felt a flicker of annoyance. How dare he come up to her room and make fun of her?

Dane saw the look on her face, and his green eyes turned serious. "I am in a band, Emily," he said. "It's called Pop Smear."

She winced. "That's disgusting."

"Yeah, I know. It was the only name we could agree on, though." He shrugged. "Anyway, I also take classes at the university, and I thought we could walk together. When is your first class?"

"Not until noon," Emily lied. For some reason, she didn't want to walk to her very first college class with this guy. He was too sarcastic. She wanted to be able to enjoy her first day.

"Oh, that's too bad," Dane said, making no move to leave.

"Well, good night," Emily said awkwardly.

He looked at her. His eyes were so *green*.

He wears tinted contact lenses, she thought. *Nobody except a cat has eyes that green.*

"Yes, good night," Dane said. There was something in his voice that Emily didn't like at all. She remembered the insolent way he'd looked at her when he said, "There is a God," as though she was pretty for his benefit or something.

Never Fall in Love

He thinks it's just a matter of time before I come around and fall in love with him, she thought, disgusted. *Well, sorry, but that's not going to happen, guy.*

Dane was still watching her. He seemed to take note of whatever emotions were playing across her face, and smiled. "Good night," he said again, and walked slowly across her room and out the door.

Emily blew out her breath in irritation. There was something so arrogant about him. *As though I would ever fall for him,* she thought.

She pulled on a nightgown and climbed into bed. She shifted around, trying to get comfortable. She could hear the sounds of traffic outside, and the creaking, settling sounds of the house.

Suddenly she sat up, straining her ears. From far away she could hear someone playing the guitar. Dane, to be specific. She sighed in exasperation. He knew she was just about to go to bed. She debated putting on her robe and stomping through the house to tell him to be quiet, but there was something too housemotherish about that image, so she stayed where she was.

She listened for another moment, frowning, then a small twinkle touched her eyes. Dane was playing "Good Night, Irene."

She lay back down. Above her in the attic, Mac was moving around restlessly in his Rollerblades. They made a sandpapery sliding sound that she found rather soothing.

Eventually she couldn't hear the sound of the Rollerblades anymore, and she listened to the patter of Mac's feet as he got ready for bed. Then Dane's guitar stopped, and even the house quieted down, its creakings and moanings growing less and less frequent until one by one they died out, and Emily fell asleep.

Chapter 4

"GET OUT OF THE SHOWER already!" Emily shouted cheerfully to Holly the next morning as she brushed her teeth in their shared bathroom.

"Don't you dare spit into the sink from across the room!" Holly responded affectionately from the shower.

Mac, embarrassed, skulked in the hallway, wearing a towel and waiting patiently for them to finish.

On the floor below, Michael rose an hour early in order to be out of the bathroom before Paris could possibly want in. A green silk robe— Paris's—was hanging on the back of the bathroom door. He touched the sleeve gently.

In the basement, Dane showered in the little stall near the washer and dryer. Its walls were gray cement, its floor was pebbly, and it had an ancient plastic shower curtain.

"Wow," Dane said a few minutes later, bouncing into the kitchen, wearing only jeans, his narrow bare chest still damp. Emily, Holly, Michael, and Paris were gathered around the table. "That is the world's most depressing shower. It's like I'm in prison and this is my one shower per week. I probably should've done push-ups, since it's safe to break a sweat on Mondays."

Paris wrinkled her nose. "Where do you come up with this stuff?"

Dane shrugged. "I watched a lot of prison movies when I was small, which is why I play the guitar."

Michael turned sideways in his chair. "You play the guitar because of prison movies?"

Dane nodded. "My mother wouldn't let me play the harmonica because convicts in prison movies always play the harmonica, and she said, 'Look what harmonica playing leads to, Dane,' and—"

"This is not a true story," Emily broke in.

Dane fixed his gaze on her. She was wearing a cream-colored sweater, and her hair fell to her shoulders in rich waves. But her black eyebrows were drawn together, making a startling line against her pale skin.

"I guarantee this is not a true story," she said firmly.

Dane grinned. "You're right."

"I think the best stories are untrue stories," Holly said softly.

Dane looked at her appreciatively. "I think so, too, Holly." He glanced around the table at them. "My, my," he said mockingly. "Look at the clean and shining faces, ready for the first day of school. Has everyone packed their lunch boxes?"

"Stop making fun of us," Emily snapped, her cheeks flushing. "I'm so sorry you—"

"How can I not make fun of four people sitting around a dining table," Dane interrupted smoothly, "waiting for someone to serve them breakfast in a house where the cupboards are bare, except for maybe a tea bag?"

"We aren't waiting for breakfast," Emily said through clenched teeth. She indicated the notebook and pencil lying on the table. "We're making the dinner schedule and shopping list."

"Really?" Dane raised his eyebrows. "When do we start, and who's first?"

"I am," Holly said miserably. "Can you believe I have to go tomorrow?"

"Oh, it'll be okay," Dane told her. "You can make oatmeal and we'll continue with the prison cellblock theme. You can stand by the pot and we'll all file through, shuffling and swearing, and—"

Emily pushed back her chair with a screech. "I have to go to class," she said shortly, picking up her backpack.

Dane checked his watch. "Leaving pretty early for a noon class, aren't you?" he asked, grinning.

Emily glared at him, then silently pushed out the door.

After Dane, Paris, and Michael left for campus, Holly sat at the dining room table alone, suddenly blue. The School of the Arts was housed in a separate building away from the main campus, so she couldn't walk to class with everyone else. Her first class wasn't for another hour anyway.

Holly leaned forward and rested her cheek against the scarred mahogany of the table, thinking about how noisy and lively the room had been a moment ago. Not that it was a completely *good* kind of lively, at least as far as Holly was concerned. It didn't exactly make Holly feel comfortable to see Mac *and* Dane apparently crazy about her best friend.

We've been here twenty-four hours and two guys are in love with her already, Holly thought glumly. *In fact, the only two guys we've met are in love with her. I wonder what would've happened if another guy had moved in instead of Paris?*

Yeah, and what about Paris, anyway? Holly had never seen someone so glamorous. That morning Paris had been wearing tweed pants and a pale green sweater set, like the ones Holly's grandmother had worn in photos taken in the fifties, and a matching pale green beret. Holly could never pull off an outfit like that. First of all, her head was too small, and hats always slid too far down on her forehead until she was peeking out from beneath them, as if she were wearing a bank teller's visor or something. Second, she could never wear something as retro as a sweater set without feeling totally self-conscious, like someone dressed up for Halloween.

But Paris had looked completely at ease—and completely gorgeous. Michael had pulled out her chair when she sat down at the dining room table. He had pulled out a chair for Paris in her own house! The only people who ever pulled out chairs for Holly were waiters in fancy restaurants. Holly thought about the no-dating rule. Somehow she didn't think it applied to Michael and Paris.

So, let's see . . . Michael and Paris liked each other, Mac and Dane both liked Emily, but who liked Holly? They all liked her, she was sure. They all just loved her as a friend. But no one liked her as more than that.

Emily had said that she didn't want college to be a repeat of high school. Well, neither did Holly. In high school, she and Emily used to go to the public library together, and while guys would ask Emily out, old people would ask Holly how to use the card catalog. It was the story of her life. She wished the story would improve.

"Hey," said a voice behind her. "If you're that sleepy, go back to bed."

Holly lifted her head. Mac was standing in the doorway, smiling at her.

"Listen," he said, "I'm about to go to work. Why don't I walk you to the arts building on my way?"

Holly considered. There were certainly worse things than walking to class with a handsome guy—even if he was in love with her best friend.

She pushed her hair off her forehead. "That would be lovely," she said.

Michael sat in Organic Chemistry, almost dozing in the rays of late-morning sunshine that streamed through the large window. Although his mind was pleasantly drowsy, his hand took rapid notes. That was the secret to Michael's good grades: he could translate what any teacher said into an immediate outline, neatly, precisely, and without concentrating. Three months earlier, when he graduated from high school, a girl he hardly knew had come up to him and shaken his hand. "I've sat next to you in history for four years," she'd said. "I would have failed if it hadn't been for your notes."

Sometimes Michael wondered what would happen when he stopped being a student. There weren't a lot of professions that demanded good note-taking abilities. Well, maybe a court stenographer. He debated his future career as a court stenographer with one corner of his mind, while another part, one that had been at work constantly in the past twenty-four hours, thought about Paris.

That part of his brain was trying to decide how much he liked her. She was without a doubt the prettiest girl he had ever met. And she had a personality, too. The only problem was that he wasn't so sure it was a *nice* personality. For instance, this morning she had talked to Holly for about twenty minutes about art school, and then as soon as they left the house, she'd said, "Isn't Holly coming with us?" and Michael had had to explain that Holly went to the arts building. Did Paris think about frozen waffles while other people talked?

The teacher stopped talking, and Michael realized that he'd written "Class dismissed" in his notes. He erased it, gathered up his books, and went outside, blinking in the bright noon sunshine.

It took a few minutes for his brain to return to normal everyday functioning, and he strolled along campus in a pleasant haze for some time before he saw Paris ahead of him. She was talking to a tall guy with glasses, the breeze fluttering her long, straight hair.

Cautiously Michael walked closer, wondering if this was Paris's boyfriend. But Paris saw him over the guy's shoulder and bounded over.

"Hi, Michael." She held her books to her chest with one hand. She had a half-eaten sandwich in the other. "So . . . how were classes? How do you like campus? Have you seen any of the others? Do you want a bite of my sandwich?"

Michael decided to answer only the last question. "Yes, please," he said.

She smiled and held out the sandwich. He took a bite. It was cream cheese and olives. He chewed and swallowed. "That was really disgusting."

She laughed. "Well, you should have asked what it was if you were so concerned."

"Yeah, well, I would've if I'd known that anyone besides my mother actually eats those," Michael responded. "I thought it was something that she made up." He grinned at Paris. The green sweater made her blue eyes look turquoise. "Why don't we go have some real food?"

She shook her head. "I can't. It would violate the dreaded no-dating house rule, after all. Plus Rick's waiting for me." She gestured behind her and took a bite of her sandwich.

Michael glanced over her shoulder and saw that the tall guy was patiently waiting. *Oh, right,* he thought, feeling like an idiot. He'd forgotten all about that guy.

He looked at Paris again and felt an unexpected tingle of pleasure. "You have cream cheese on the corner of your mouth."

"*Gross,*" said Paris, catching the dab of cheese with her small pink tongue.

Emily had calmed down by the time noon rolled around. In her ten o'clock class, Human Communications, they had had to form groups, and now Emily sat on the grass in front of the student union with two members of her group, Becky and Sandra, eating sandwiches from the cafeteria.

"What did you say your major was, Emily?" Sandra asked, taking a bite of her sandwich. She had short black hair and a pretty, gamine face.

"Environmental science right now," Emily responded. "But there are other classes I want to take."

"How many classes *are* you taking?" Becky asked, nodding at the printout of Emily's schedule, which lay on the grass. "It looks like about a thousand credit hours."

"Six classes, twenty-two credits," Emily admitted.

Becky and Sandra shrieked in mock horror.

"You're crazy," Sandra said.

"Certifiable," Becky added.

Emily shifted self-consciously on the grass. "I

just— I want to get a lot out of my education," she explained.

"Yeah, well, that's great," Sandra said. "But it might be nice if you didn't have a stroke your first semester here—" She broke off suddenly, a smile lighting her pretty face. "Hi, Dane!" she called.

Emily turned. Dane was walking slowly past them. He'd put on a ragged flannel shirt, and the red bandanna was around his head again.

"Oh, hello," he said, smiling at Sandra. "Hi, Emily."

Emily barely nodded. She'd managed to forget about Dane for a moment there. Was he going to dog her every step?

"Do you want to join us?" Becky asked.

Emily crushed her sandwich wrapper into a ball. If Dane sat down, she would stand up.

Dane raised his eyebrows at the crumpled wrapper. "Thanks, but I don't think Emily wants me to. See you around."

As he walked off, Sandra glanced at Emily, a small frown on her face. "Jeez, why were you so mean?"

Emily bit her lip, suddenly ashamed. Why *had* she been so obviously rude? Dane was only being friendly.

Sandra was still looking at her. "How do you know him, anyway?" she asked.

Emily rolled her shoulders uncomfortably. "He's my housemate," she said awkwardly. She felt as though she were admitting something extremely personal, like he was her AA sponsor or something.

"Wow, you are so lucky," Sandra said. "He knows your name and everything."

"Well, you said hello to him," Emily pointed out. "Don't you guys know each other?"

"Actually, we haven't exactly been introduced," Sandra said. "I just know his name because of the band."

"*Everyone* knows his name because of the band," Becky said. "Every girl, at least."

Emily practically choked on her sandwich. "He's popular with girls?"

Becky and Sandra stared at her. "Exceptionally," Becky said. "Why are you so surprised? Don't you think he's adorable?"

"Not exactly," said Emily, who had not used the word *adorable* to describe a boy since she was fourteen or so. She checked her watch. "I have to go to my next class," she said, standing up.

As she walked away from the union she spotted Michael. Emily could find Michael a mile away, no matter how huge the crowd was—that was how well she knew him, how quickly she heard the rasp of his voice, how easily she recognized his gait. Once she had spotted him in the crowd during a televised football game.

Now she saw him standing on the sidewalk, sharing a sandwich with a girl in a green beret. Paris. Emily wrinkled her nose. She hoped Michael wasn't falling for Paris. She was so cold. Beautiful, yes, but cold.

Emily shrugged off the thought. She should trust him to have better taste. *He's definitely too good for Paris, and he knows it,* she decided, heading for class.

Holly thought Mac was well behaved on the walk to class—that is, he didn't talk about how great he thought Emily was. He may have been *thinking* about it, but at least he didn't blather on about his heart's desire.

Instead, he kept the conversation going in the manner she found so soothing, asking her lots of nice closed-ended questions about Rollerblading. When they got near the arts building, he pointed it out, and then, after asking her if she was sure she could find her way home, turned and went into Sports City.

Holly wasn't really nervous about attending her first college class. Actually, art class was one of the few places where Holly felt at home. It was a place where she understood what was expected of her, where she could predict the behavior of others, where she knew what to do.

But that day when she entered her first class, Life Drawing, everyone else looked so tense that Holly felt anxious, too. She saw the reason immediately.

A beautiful black woman in a short, sheer robe sat on the model's platform in the middle of the room.

She nodded to Holly. "I think everyone's here," she said. "Will you shut the door?"

"Sure," Holly whispered. She closed the door.

"Thank you," the woman said. She untied the

belt of her robe. "My name is Isabelle," she said, shrugging out of the robe as casually as though she were writing her name on the chalkboard. "I'm your model today. Your teacher asked me to have you do charcoal sketches until she arrives."

Holly lowered her eyes to the floor, a little embarrassed, but nodded. Quickly Holly took her place at an easel as the other students fanned out to easels around the room as well.

So much for not being nervous. Holly's hands were shaking so badly, she could barely hold the charcoal. She had worked with models before, many times, but never in a roomful of strangers, and never with a model this beautiful.

But her confidence returned as she began to draw. Isabelle was glorious; she was a joy to sketch. She had beautifully defined shoulders sloping to firm, full breasts, a small waist, and a flat stomach. Her legs were gently, perfectly muscled. But it was her face that caught and held Holly's attention: her hair was cropped close, showing the perfect line of her skull, and she had lovely deep-set black eyes with long lashes, sharp cheekbones, and full, rosy lips.

It's her face and legs that I'd like to draw, Holly thought. So she drew Isabelle from a bird's-eye view. In her drawing, Isabelle's face was upturned, as though someone had called to her from above, and you could just make out the angle of her breasts, and then her legs, visible from the thigh down and extended, as though she were flexing them playfully.

"That's just fantastic." The voice startled Holly,

who had been retouching the toes. It was Isabelle, back in her robe. "I wish I looked that good in real life."

"Oh, um, th-thanks," Holly stammered, not sure how to respond. She wasn't used to having models come over to examine her sketch of them.

Isabelle took Holly's sketchpad and tore off the page. "Excellent," she said again.

Holly looked up to see everyone's eyes on her and the model.

Isabelle smiled. "Well, that's it for today."

Holly frowned. She was new at this college art student thing, but she hadn't expected the model to run the class.

Obviously other students were thinking the same thing. "Excuse me, but isn't the teacher going to show up?" a girl with long red hair asked.

Isabelle smiled again. "What I neglected to tell you was that I'm your teacher as well as your model. You all did very well today. I'll see you again on Wednesday."

And she went striding from the room, Holly's sketch firmly in her hand.

Chapter 5

EMILY LEANED AGAINST THE kitchen counter, keeping Holly company as she finished making that night's dinner—three giant omelets and a big platter of home fries.

Holly fidgeted with the spices and silverware, repeating for the seventh or eighth time the reasons she had chosen this particular menu. "Well, you know how I hate handling raw meat. I mean, working in a chicken restaurant will do that to you, right? And since none of us had breakfast this morning, having breakfast food for dinner might sort of balance the day out." She looked at Emily anxiously, wringing her hands. "Right?"

Emily laughed. "Chill, sweet pea. Everything looks great."

Everything did look great. The omelets turned out nice and fluffy and golden. Holly set them on the table and called the others to dinner. They trooped in noisily, Michael from his room, Dane pounding up the basement stairs, Mac flying in the door on his Rollerblades, a light film of perspiration on his face.

"Where's Paris?" Holly asked once everyone was seated.

"She's in the shower," Michael answered casually. "Let's go ahead. She'll be down in a minute."

Holly watched apprehensively as Dane served himself a piece of omelet. "Mushrooms," he said. "Excellent."

Emily shot Holly a look that said, *See, nothing to worry about.* Holly smiled a little.

"I'm starving," Mac said. "I didn't even get a lunch break today because some man was buying skis for his, like, two wives and seven children."

"Well, I've been stuck in anatomy lab all afternoon," Michael said. "Think what *that* was like."

Holly set down her fork. "Please don't tell us, Michael."

He winked at her. "We have visitors' day in October. You can come see for yourself." He took a bite of his omelet. "I'm glad that you didn't make liver or kidneys or tongue, though."

"I ate a whole platter of tongue at a party once," Dane said. "I thought it was roast beef."

Emily looked at him. "How could you have thought it was roast beef?"

"Well, I didn't think it was *good* roast beef," Dane clarified. "But I was cornered near the buffet, talking to this really boring woman, and so I kept eating pieces and thinking, boy, this is not very good roast beef, and then the really boring woman said, 'They serve the best tongue here, don't you think?' and I said, 'The best *what?*' and—"

Emily sighed and turned away just as Paris breezed into the dining room, barefoot, wearing jeans and a T-shirt. Her blond hair was shower-damp and tangled.

She probably had to take a shower because she was all scratchy from that cashmere sweater set, Emily thought sarcastically, then tried to push the thought away. Why was she so down on Paris? After all, she barely knew her.

Paris, who was managing to exude a fair amount of allure despite having gotten out of the shower two minutes before, surveyed the table. "Is this breakfast or dinner?" she asked with a hint of disdain.

Emily saw Holly wince.

That's why I'm so down on Paris, Emily thought. *Because she's so mean.*

Paris sat down and helped herself to a piece of omelet and a few potatoes.

"Are you going to eat those?" Mac said, pointing to the potatoes remaining on the platter.

Paris gave him a faintly incredulous look. "I don't know," she said. "I haven't even eaten the ones I put on my plate yet."

"Because I want them if you don't."

"There's more in the kitchen," Holly said.

"Really?" Mac said, his face lighting up with genuine pleasure. He jumped up and took his plate into the kitchen. "Oh, wow," he called. "Is this dessert for us, too?"

Holly laughed. "Gosh, I'd completely forgotten about it. I bought a cheesecake at the bakery," she explained to everyone at the table.

Emily relaxed, glad someone appreciated Holly's efforts. Mac was so . . . *nice,* always saying or doing the perfect thing.

Paris was eating her potatoes happily. "I'm so hungry," she said. "All I had for lunch was half a sandwich."

Emily glanced at Michael. He was casually folding his napkin into tiny squares. Emily frowned. Wouldn't now be the perfect moment for Michael to agree with Paris? To say, "Yeah, I ate the other half," or whatever? But as Holly brought out the cheesecake Michael kept his eyes on his plate.

They don't want us to know they saw each other on campus, Emily thought. She felt a pinprick of something, half jealousy, half possessiveness.

"I have to go," Dane said suddenly. "Someone's coming over. Save me a piece of cheesecake, will you, Holly?"

"Sure," Holly said.

Emily watched Dane stand up and stretch. She remembered Sandra and Becky talking that afternoon, and she tried to look at him objectively. Was he "adorable"?

Well, he had even features, and his skin was a smooth hazel brown, and of course he had nice eyes. But that perpetual greasy red bandanna . . . and the goatee. How could someone be attractive with a goatee?

Not even Woodrow Wilson pulled that off, and he was President, Emily thought.

Why was she thinking about this, anyway? Just because a couple of fluffy-headed girls thought Dane was attractive, did she have to start reevaluating him? Was she that superficial? Besides, did Dane's looks even come close to making up for his appalling personality?

Emily speared a large chunk of cheesecake with her fork and pushed thoughts of Dane from her mind.

They had drawn up the kitchen roster that morning, and Michael had been secretly pleased that both he and Paris were on dish duty that night, but he was even happier about it now.

He had never known that doing dishes could be so wonderful. Paris was washing, he was rinsing. Every time she handed him a plate or a glass, her fingers slipped over his, slowly, deliberately. They kept up a steady stream of boring small talk so the others wouldn't notice anything.

"How many classes did you have today?" Michael asked loudly. Paris touched his wrist with her soapy finger. His mouth was dry as cotton.

"Just one," Paris answered lightly. "Beginning Drama."

"Oh," Michael said. He took a glass from her and slowly twined his fingers with hers. He struggled for something to say. "I was in a play in high school."

"Really?" Paris said. "Which one?"

"*Oedipus Rex,*" Michael said. "I was the Greek chorus."

"The whole chorus?"

"Well, it was a limited production," Michael said. He was staring at Paris. Her face was glowing from the heat of the dishwater, and small beads of sweat clung to her hairline. She smiled her generous smile. There was not one feature of her face Michael would have improved upon.

"We're done," she said.

"What?"

"The dishes." She indicated the stacked dish drainer. "We're done."

"Oh," Michael said. He wondered what would happen now. Should he suggest they go for a walk? To a movie? To his room?

"Good night," Paris said, walking toward the kitchen door.

"Hey, where are you going?" Michael asked.

"To bed," Paris said. "To sleep." And she did.

Emily was in her room, trying to study. She was reading the first chapter in her political science textbook, using a pink highlighter to mark the important points. She glanced back and saw that she had highlighted every word of the last three pages without even realizing it.

She sighed and shut the book. Maybe it was thinking about Dane that was still distracting her. *Well, not exactly thinking about Dane,* she corrected herself. Thinking about how rude she'd been to him. Imagine if she'd been the one walking along campus and said hello to him and he'd barely acknowledged her! She would have felt awful.

She was sure that was why she kept thinking about Dane. She was not, repeat, *not* so shallow that her new-found knowledge that Dane was a campus heartthrob would cause her to alter her opinion of him. She owed him an apology, that was all. Well, once she had apologized, she could put it out of her mind.

She pushed back her chair and pattered swiftly down the stairs. She paused at the bottom, wondering if she should have run a comb through her hair, then frowned sharply. She was going to give him a brief apology, not enter a beauty contest.

She walked quietly through the kitchen, not wanting anyone to hear her going down to Dane's room. She opened the door to the basement. She could hear music playing softly. "Dane?" she called shyly. There was no answer.

She crept halfway down the stairs and called again. Still no answer. Maybe he was studying.

She reached the bottom of the stairs and entered the doorless arch to Dane's room.

"Dane, can I talk to—"

The couple on the couch pulled apart abruptly.

"Oh, my God," Emily said, backing away. Her face flushed crimson. "I'm sorry, I—"

"Hi, Emily," said the girl.

"Hello," Emily said awkwardly. Then she looked at the girl for the first time. "Sandra?"

Sandra smoothed her short black hair. "Nice to see you again," she said, unconcerned. She turned to Dane. "Listen, I should be going anyway," she said.

Dane's eyes were on Emily. He looked very amused. "Okay," he said. "I'll see you later."

Sandra leaned over and kissed him quickly. "It's a deal," she said.

She brushed by Emily and up the stairs.

"Aren't you going to walk her to her car?" Emily said, edging closer to the staircase.

Dane shrugged. "She knows the way, I imagine." He smiled. "What was it you wanted to talk to me about?"

Emily lifted her chin. "Nothing," she said, turning to leave.

"Hey, wait a minute," Dane said. "You barge in here, interrupt my date—"

"Date?" Emily said. She crossed her arms. Her face was still pink with embarrassment. "*Date?* You didn't even know her name this afternoon! I know, she told me. And now you—" She broke off, cringing as she recalled that she had actually thought Dane might be *studying* too hard to hear her.

"She caught up with me outside the library and introduced herself then," Dane said mildly.

"Oh, so you've known each other for hours," Emily said sarcastically. "I'm sorry I leaped to conclusions."

"Why do you care, anyway?" Dane said.

"What?"

"Why do you care? What difference could it possibly make to you how long I've known Sonia?"

"Sandra!"

"Whatever."

"Oh, you are impossible! I was right about you all along! I should never have—" She stopped abruptly.

Dane raised his eyebrows. "You should never have what?" He smiled. "Were you coming down here to tell me something special?"

Emily wondered how she had so completely lost control of this conversation. "I wasn't."

"You were, and you walked in on us, and now you're jealous."

"I'm not jealous."

"I'm sorry," Dane said with maddening sincerity. "I didn't know you were the possessive type, or I would have never let Sonia come over."

"*Sandra!*" Emily practically screamed. "And I'm not jealous!"

"You don't have to deny it."

"I'm *not* jealous," Emily said slowly and deliberately. "What are you, deaf?"

"Actually, yes, a little bit," Dane said thoughtfully. "In the right ear."

Chapter 6

THE MAIL AT 28 SPRUCE STREET
was, like mail everywhere, greatly anticipated even
though nobody ever received anything exciting.

Actually, that was not completely true. Holly
received many letters, because like a lot of lonely
people, she had cultivated many pen pals over the
years. One of these pen pals was a man who had
made such a career out of letter-writing that he'd
actually had to quit his job as an insurance agent
just to keep up. *60 Minutes* had interviewed him
once, and he admitted that he had over a thousand pen pals. Holly, who saw the episode, had
been horrified. A thousand pen pals! It hardly
seemed worth writing to him. (Plus Holly was
almost certain she could see flecks of food in his
beard. How could the producers have let him on
national television like that?) But she was unsure
how to stop.

Dane also got quite a bit of mail because he
corresponded with other musicians whose
addresses he got out of the back of *Melody Maker*.

These letters were sporadic and unreliable, often written in pencil on wrinkled pieces of brown paper bag. But they were often technical and usually helpful: *I have found that moving the index finger first can increase the speed of the Tennessee shift.* . . . Dane received a fair number of letters like this, and everyone in the house would have screamed with laughter had they known. In fact, Dane would have found the whole thing tremendously mockable if the addressee had been anyone other than himself.

Emily's mail consisted mainly of greeting cards because she was the kind of bright, thoughtful girl to whom relatives and friends like to send greeting cards. Granted, the relatives were typically stuck in, oh, 1978, and the cards had pictures of apple-cheeked children in pinafores, and the inscriptions read, "To a wonderful little girl . . ." And the cards from friends tended to be long, boring accounts of their various heartbreaks, but mail is mail and Emily didn't complain.

Mac's mail was almost all postcards from friends at various ski resorts. The most memorable of these was from a ski instructor at Buttermilk who'd probably fallen down and hit his head a few too many times, because on the back he'd written, "I skied this totally gnarly incline today."

Paris had received so many love letters in her life that she could conceivably have looked forward to the mail's holding some real excitement. But most of the love letters had bored her. She had read them dispassionately, mentally correcting grammar and spelling mistakes. She could have told anyone who asked that *friend* was the most misspelled word in love letters, inevitably appearing as *freind*.

Michael never received letters from anyone because he was the most infrequent of correspondents and the most wooden of writers. Even his thank-you letters read like a textbook: "Thank you for the gift. It was very nice. . . ."

As it happened, this particular morning three members of the household received personal letters of some significance, but that was surely an exception. The mothers of everyone in the house would have said that the decline and fall of written correspondence can be attributed to the temptation of telephones, and that letter-writing is a dying art, and that young people are so lazy these days, but I myself am not so sure.

Emily sat on the bus, reading her letter. It was from Frank.

> Dear Emily,
>   Well, here I am all settled in at the U of M, missing you. My roommate is pretty nice, although he has hung Grateful Dead posters all over the place and he keeps telling me Grateful Dead facts, such as "they're the sixth richest rock group in the world." I don't know if this is true or not.
>   Em, I can't believe you meant what you said to me at the airport about wanting to see other people. Sure, parting is hard, but

we can make it work. I mean, we've been through a lot, and we've always made it work, right?

Homecoming is right around the corner. I don't know how you want to work that. Do you want to come here, or shall I go there? I don't know if we can afford two plane tickets, but maybe if we ask our parents for part of our Christmas presents . . .

There was more, but Emily didn't read it. She was too angry. Of course she'd meant what she'd said at the airport! She felt like crying when she remembered how hard she'd had to maneuver to get Frank alone, out of his parents' clutches. She'd had the speech about seeing other people prepared and rehearsed for five *days,* and now Frank simply didn't believe her!

She considered tearing Frank's letter up into small pieces and letting them slip out the window, but that would be littering. Plus she was afraid the bus driver would yell at her. Instead she stuffed it into her backpack, where it would haunt her all day until she felt compelled to finish it and then she'd just be angrier and—

Emily gasped.

Frank had just climbed onto the bus at the Darley Avenue stop.

She closed her eyes, heart pounding. She counted to five and opened them again. She sighed with relief. It wasn't really Frank, but it sure looked like him: tall, sandy-haired, cleft chin, pale blue eyes. And worst of all, this guy was wearing a tan sweater vest *and* had a pencil stuck behind his ear. The real Frank was actually a fairly natty dresser, but Emily had always sensed a nerdier, more studious side lurking somewhere.

The fake Frank lurched down the aisle and, sure enough, sat next to her. Emily examined his profile out of the corner of her eye. Same determined jaw, same straight nose, different mouth.

For no particular reason, Emily remembered how when Frank ate dinner at her house, he used to rearrange the seating so it was boy-girl, boy-girl. (He actually said that. If she and Frank had had children, they would've hated him.) And then *during* dinner, he would talk endlessly with her father about her father's old football days until Emily felt as if she would scream.

Suddenly she could take it no more. She scrambled out of her seat, past the fake Frank, causing him to drop his books. She darted to the front of the bus and, not knowing exactly where it had stopped, got off.

She stood there breathing heavily as the bus pulled away. Then she began walking, staring at the ground and scuffing her feet. She caught her breath and tried to laugh at herself. She was being such an idiot.

She kept walking, reading street signs, trying to orient herself. What was so horrible about someone who looked like Frank? What, in fact, was so monstrously horrible about Frank himself? He was just someone who loved her, she supposed. Now that she was on the subject, what was so horrible about Dane? And Mac? And Paris and all the others? Suddenly Emily wondered where she would end up if she didn't stop rejecting people.

She looked around and tried to figure out where she was. An emotion in her chest bubbled ominously close to tears. It was a lot like homesickness, but it was something else.

Paris took a later bus, which rumbled right by Emily as she trudged along dispiritedly. But Paris was reading a letter of her own and therefore didn't notice.

Paris's letter was from her stepmother.

Dearest P—

Your father asked me to send you this check. We are so happy you found such a nice place to live.

Love,
Marilyn

Enclosed was a pale blue check for two thousand dollars. Paris folded the check and put it in her wallet. She stuffed the letter from her stepmother into the crack between the seat and the window.

We are so happy . . . Paris sighed in annoyance.

If my father's so happy, why doesn't he call and tell me that? she thought irritably. *Why make Marilyn write me that mealymouthed note? Does it ever occur to anyone that I might want some human contact?*

She supposed she could call and talk to

Marilyn, but Marilyn would just be all sugary and insincere. *Oh, a condemned house?* she would say. *Is that wise, dear? Of course your father and I trust you completely, but . . .*

Or Paris could call her mother, provided she could have her mother paged in the sanitarium. But her mother would say, *Paris? Sweetest? Are you coming to see me? Soon? You promise? Hold on—I have to get my Scotch bottle.* Of course, she probably wouldn't say that part about the Scotch bottle, but that was the general idea.

Or Paris could call her father at the office, but he would say, *Is something wrong?* and she'd say, *Well, no . . .* and he'd say, *Honey, I have eight million people here who need my attention. . . .* If she said she just wanted to talk, he would sigh and remind her of all the things that had to be paid for: her BMW, and his Mercedes, and Marilyn's Mercedes, and the new house, and the swimming pool, and college tuition, and on and on.

Which was part of why Paris had wanted to move into the house on Spruce Street, because she thought that people would naturally be closer when money wasn't such an issue. She thought, though she would never have admitted it, that she'd be part of a group there, like a family with lots of brothers and sisters. Paris had always wanted lots of brothers and sisters.

But it was sure turning out to be a lot of *bother*. Emily and her stupid meal plan, for example. And that ridiculous dishwashing rotation. Plus the only other girls in the house had been best friends since the cradle. As for Mac and Dane—well, Paris couldn't quite picture herself having a big heart-to-heart conversation with Mac while he waxed his skis, or shouting to Dane while he rehearsed in the basement. Which left Michael, and Paris wasn't sure how she felt about Michael . . .

And so Paris got off the bus on campus, far ahead of Emily but no less alone.

Emily came home from class and Dane popped out of the kitchen, a frilly apron tied over his jeans and ripped T-shirt.

"Hold it right there!" he cried.

"What?" Emily asked nervously, backing toward the door. Was there a fire in the kitchen?

"Just a minute," he said, darting back into the kitchen. He reappeared holding a tray with a plate of peanut butter cookies and a glass of milk. He set the tray on the dining room table and patted the seat of a chair.

"Come on," he said, taking a seat himself. "Tell me all about your day at school." He leaned forward, looking so interested and expectant—and so very much like her mother—that Emily laughed.

She sat down. "Well," she said, "I had sociology today, and—"

"Drink your milk," Dane urged in true motherly fashion. "Have a cookie, dear."

Emily took a bite of one of the cookies. "Wow." She looked at him with surprise. "These are fantastic."

74

Dane's green eyes sparkled with pleasure. "Well, my mother's a home ec teacher," he said. "Of course I bake good cookies."

"Really?" Emily said. "Do you cook whole meals this well, too?"

"Naw." Dane shook his head. "I do make pretty good crab cakes, though. My mother always starts the cooking semester by trying to perfect her crab cake recipe, and by the time she's frittered away six weeks on that she has to skip straight to dessert."

Emily began eating another cookie. "Was it hard to have your mother teaching at your school?"

"Are you kidding? She wasn't at my school," Dane responded. "But I used to do guest appearances in her classes every year. I would play the guitar, and all the students would serve me crab cakes. My mother was trying to boost my career." He looked thoughtful. "It was incredibly pathetic, now that I think about it. What do you think she said before I got there? 'Now, everyone, music is very important to Dane, so be sure to clap really, really hard.'"

The kitchen door slammed as Paris came in. She looked hot and irritable, but beautiful nonetheless. Her blue eyes took in the scene at the table. "Oh, spare me," she said. "I do not have the stomach for Emily's goody-goody act today."

She brushed past them, and they heard her swear briefly as she dropped one of her books. She picked it up and tramped up the stairs.

Emily set her cookie down; suddenly she'd lost

her taste for them. She looked at Dane across the table. He looked back at her and shrugged.

"Well, I'd better get going," she said, standing up stiffly, because the mood was shattered like Emily's grandmother's turkey platter, which Emily had dropped when she was seven years old, and which could never be repaired.

Holly had spotted the art gallery the day before, but she hadn't had the opportunity to go in until now. She paused at the door. "O'Halloran Showcase," said a sign in the window. Holly entered, and a small bell jingled over the door.

The gallery was horribly disorganized. Dusty boxes were stacked on one side of the narrow room. A few paintings were hung on the opposite wall, and more were stacked on the floor. Farther back, two giant, poorly lit glass cases held jewelry displays.

No one was standing by the cash register or sitting behind the cluttered oak desk, so Holly toured the paintings displayed at the front of the store. She strolled from one to the next, examining them carefully.

She thought the artist had talent, but tended to be too cutesy. The animals had cherubic, happy faces. But she liked the ones without animals— one of a vase of daffodils, in particular. And one of an empty kitchen was good, although Holly mentally erased a child's red shoe from the corner of the room.

Her face changed as she examined the paintings;

her usual preoccupied, dreamy look disappeared. She was focused, her brown eyes sharp and alert, her small form radiating confidence. Holly herself was unaware of the change that came over her, but it was not lost on the man who climbed up the stairs from the storage room. He was a tall man of about forty, broad-shouldered, with a handsome face and a slightly shaggy brown beard. If asked to describe him in a single word, you might choose *appealing*. His brown eyes were thoughtful as he watched the slight girl study each painting.

It was perhaps five minutes before Holly felt him gazing at her. She looked up and jumped.

"Sorry," the man said. "I didn't mean to startle you."

"That's okay," Holly breathed. "How long have you been standing there?"

"Couple of minutes," the man said. "I didn't want to disturb you."

"I wish you had," Holly said, flustered.

"Why?"

"Well, because . . ." Holly hesitated, not knowing how to explain that she didn't like the idea of being watched.

"Those are my paintings," the man said quietly. "It's not often that I get to see anyone study them with such deliberation. It was out of selfishness that I didn't say anything."

"Oh," Holly said softly. "Well, I like them." She thought it would be presumptuous to say more; it would sound as if she thought she was an art critic or something.

The man smiled. "Thank you." He held out a hand. "I'm Alan O'Halloran," he said, "and I assume you're here about the job."

"Job?" Holly repeated.

Mr. O'Halloran nodded toward the door. Holly turned and saw for the first time that a Help Wanted sign hung in the window.

"Actually, I just came in," Holly said. "I didn't even see the sign. I—I tend to be in another world part of the time."

Mr. O'Halloran laughed. "Well, at least you're honest about it. What's your name, by the way?"

Holly realized that she hadn't shaken the hand he was still holding out. "Holly Wright," she said, blushing. She could feel even her ears blush.

Mr. O'Halloran shook her hand at last. "Well, it's nice to meet you, no matter why you came here," he said. He sat down behind the large, cluttered desk. "Please browse as long as you like." He began sorting through some papers.

Holly studied another painting for a moment, this one of an empty swing. She wondered what kind of job opening there was at the gallery. She'd like to work here, she mused. She examined the painting for a moment longer, then it suddenly occurred to her that she could actually apply for the job. She might even get it. She was in college, after all. She was a free agent in Boulder. And if this man turned her down, well, she never had to come back here.

"Mr. O'Halloran?" Holly said tentatively.

He looked up from the desk and smiled expectantly.

"I guess I *am* interested in the job," Holly said.

Mr. O'Halloran's smile widened, and he stroked his beard. "Well, it's just part time, in the afternoons. I need someone to help out and do inventory and ring up purchases and stuff. Have you ever worked in a gallery before?"

"Sure," lied Holly, who had worked one summer as a chicken waitress.

"Look," Mr. O'Halloran said, almost apologetically, "do you mind filling out an application? I have to show all the applications to my partner, and . . ."

"Oh, I don't mind," Holly said quickly.

Mr. O'Halloran rummaged through the mess of papers on the desk. Then he looked at her with a rueful smile. "I'm very disorganized, as you can probably tell. Can I just have you write down a few references on a piece of paper?"

Holly nodded. She took the notebook he offered her and wrote her name, address, and telephone number. After some hesitation, she wrote "Nancy McCabe, Crunch Art Gallery" and Nancy's telephone number. Nancy had been the owner of the Crunchy Chicken Restaurant.

Mr. O'Halloran took the piece of paper and glanced at it. "Crunch Gallery," he said. "I've never heard of it."

That's because I just made it up, Holly felt like saying. *Who would name a gallery Crunch?* She gave him a small smile.

"Don't look so nervous," Mr. O'Halloran said. "Anybody who looked so pensive and sweet while studying my work has a huge advantage."

Holly blushed. "Thank you," she whispered, unable to meet his eyes. She said good-bye and walked out of the shop with as much dignity as she could manage.

As she stood on the sidewalk for a minute, breathing deeply, she realized how much she wanted this job. She wanted it more than she had wanted that denim jacket back in eighth grade, the one she'd saved almost all year for.

As soon as she was out of sight, she ran all the way home and called Nancy McCabe to ask her for a vague but glowing reference.

Mac sat at the kitchen table later that night, drinking hot cocoa and reading the letter that had come for him that morning but which he hadn't seen on the kitchen counter until now.

Dear Maximilian,
    Your mother and I are pleased that you have decided to spend another year in Boulder, as we feel that it is the best place for you right now.
    If you would like to come home for Christmas, please let us know as soon as possible.
Love,
Dad

At the bottom of the letter, his mother had written: "P.S.: Sweetie, I shot a thirty-nine at the Sugar Hills golf course!"

Mac read the sentence from his mother over and over, wondering at what point she had decided to write it. Had she come striding in from the golf course, her ash-blond hair ruffled, her cheeks bright, just as his father finished the letter? Had she said, *Oh, wait a minute, I want to add something?* Or had his father given her the letter to post and she surreptitiously added her sentence? Had she, on the other hand—

"Hi, Mac," Paris said, breaking into his thoughts as she padded barefoot through the kitchen to the refrigerator. She wore an old T-shirt that had stretched a little out of shape. Her blond hair spilled over her shoulders. "I was trying to fall asleep and I got so hungry—oh, wow, frozen Oreos, my favorite," she said, poking through the freezer.

Now it so happened that those were Emily's Oreos, bought with Emily's very own money. The purchase of the Oreos had been followed by another excruciating session of housemate rule-making at which it was decided that food in packages marked "Do not eat" should not be eaten. The Oreo box was clearly marked "Do not eat," but Paris opened it and shook out four cookies anyway.

If Mac had been a different sort of person, he might have said something.

Paris ate the cookies over the sink. "Oh, this is wonderful," she said. "Delicious."

"Holly, are you downstairs?" Emily's voice came from the staircase.

Paris froze.

"No, I'm in your room, looking for you," Holly's voice called back, and the staircase creaked as Emily walked back up.

"Oh, man," Paris said, licking crumbs from her fingers. "I was almost caught by the head of the Gestapo."

Mac looked at her steadily.

"What are you staring at, Mr. Big Eyes?" she asked. "Did I insult your girlfriend?"

"Emily's not my girlfriend."

"Uh-huh," Paris said in a tone Mac couldn't interpret. She looked toward the stairs and suddenly exclaimed, "Oh, *hey!*"

"What?" Mac said, startled.

"I just remembered. Holly got a phone call, like, hours ago, and I forgot to tell her." Paris frowned. Then she shrugged. "Well, I'll write her a note and put it on the fridge. She'll just think she didn't see it." Paris rummaged in one of the kitchen drawers for pencil and paper.

Mac watched without comment as she scratched a note and clipped it to the refrigerator with a magnet.

"Well, good night, lover boy," Paris said, brushing past him. She nudged his shoulder with her hip and patted the top of his head with one of her small hands.

Mac sat at the table a moment longer, absent-mindedly rubbing the letter from his parents across his chin. Then he stood up and read the note Paris had left for Holly.

Holly,

    Mr. O'Halloran called to say that you got
the job at the gallery.

In the corner, Paris had written, "3 P.M."

Mac put his cocoa cup in the sink. It occurred
to him that Paris might do well to consider his
father's warnings about tattoos and life on the
lam.

Holly knocked on the door of the bathroom that
Michael and Paris shared. Michael opened the
door in his pajamas, toothbrush in hand.

Holly held up her own toothbrush by way of
explanation. "Can I come in and use your sink for
a minute? Emily is taking a bath in our bathroom,
trying to soak away her anger at Dane."

Michael opened the door wider. "Be my guest.
What has Dane done now?"

"You don't want to know," Holly said, squeezing
toothpaste on her toothbrush. Michael held out
his toothbrush, and she supplied him as well.
They both began brushing. "I gather he told her
some semirevolting story about a sorority on campus where the girls have to line up according to
breast size."

"Does she have a crush on him?" Michael said
with a mouthful of foam.

Holly shrugged. "Who knows? She denies it, but
there is a certain—" She spit in the sink. "—chemistry."

Michael laughed. "Paris thinks Mac likes Emily."

Holly had resumed brushing. She nodded. "I think so, too, but Emily thinks he's too much of a slacker or something."

Michael rolled his eyes and rinsed his mouth. "Well, I suppose after Frank, pretty much anyone would seem like a slacker," he said, wiping his mouth on a towel. "She's always had horrible taste in men."

Holly wished she had a brother to say that about her with such fond exasperation. *Holly has such horrible taste in men. Holly's so impetuous when it comes to men. Holly's always falling for the wrong sort.*

But nobody, brother or otherwise, ever said anything like that about Holly, because no men had ever bothered to find out what Holly's taste was.

She sighed and glanced at Michael. "I always thought you loved Frank," she said.

Michael looked up from the towel, astonished. "I didn't love him," he said. "I tolerated him. Actually, I thought he was kind of an idiot. He always called me 'sir,' like I was Emily's dad or something."

"What about your love life?" Holly asked. "Is something cooking between you and Paris?"

"Cooking?" Michael said. "You sound like my grandmother. Besides," he added, grinning, "that would be against the house rules. And you, Holly berry? Have you met anyone?"

For no reason whatsoever, Holly thought suddenly of Mr. O'Halloran saying, *Someone as sweet and pensive as you . . .*

She shook her head. "No," she said. "No one at all."

She took her toothbrush and went to bed.

As soon as Holly left, Michael locked the bathroom door and opened the cabinet under the sink. He reached past Paris's jumble of cosmetics and his own shaving kit and pulled out a thermos wrapped in an old plaid shirt. He'd considered keeping the thermos in his house but decided against it—a thermos of Scotch and milk, he felt, would somehow upset the orderly atmosphere of his room.

Michael sat on the edge of the tub and opened the thermos. He had read about the Scotch and milk mixture in a young-adult novel about a teenage alcoholic. The girl in that novel kept a thermos of Scotch and milk in her lunch box. Michael had thought it sounded appalling, but he had to admit that it worked in a pinch. Not that he was an alcoholic, he amended quickly. It was just that when he wanted a drink, he wanted a drink, and what was he supposed to do? He wasn't about to keep his thermos in the kitchen in a house where there were five other people who might polish it off at any moment. Michael didn't pause to examine his logic too closely. If he had, he might have wondered if any of the others would want a drink badly enough to settle for Scotch and *milk*.

The Scotch was burning a comfortable path to his stomach. Michael spread a towel in the bathtub and lay down. He thought about Paris.

He'd waited a discreet ten minutes after she'd left the kitchen the night before, then he'd left it himself and knocked on her door. But there had been no answer, and no sliver of light underneath the door, either. She couldn't have gone to sleep, could she? At eight-thirty? So what had she been doing? Just hiding in there and ignoring him?

Michael knew that most girls found him attractive. He was not conceited and he was not a womanizer—he simply knew that for some reason girls found his looks appealing, and that they found his attentiveness refreshing. So why was Paris resisting?

The Scotch was as soothing to Michael as hot chocolate, as flannel sheets, as chicken soup, as a childhood home. He would have been very surprised to learn that not everyone reacts that way to alcohol, that to most people drinking is social or recreational. Michael assumed that everyone loved drinking the way he did: deeply and secretly.

It was a huge thermos, and Michael drank all of its contents. He fell asleep in the bathtub, the thermos clutched in his hands, which was uncomfortable, but not as much as it appeared.

Chapter 7

"HOLLY, WILL YOU PLEASE TAKE A break?" Mr. O'Halloran said at noon. "You're going to collapse of exhaustion otherwise, and I'll have to answer to the Board of Health or the artists' union or something."

Holly positioned a painting on a hanger. "I just want to hang this last painting," she said.

The gallery had been transformed. Holly had persuaded Mr. O'Halloran to help her drag all the miscellaneous cartons and boxes from the front of the shop down to the storeroom. Of course, first they had to take all the old newspapers and scraps of wood and lengths of pipe *out* of the storeroom. Then, while Mr. O'Halloran unpacked his cartons (which had been in the front of the gallery for ten *months*) and created something resembling an organized storage area, Holly had vacuumed the gallery floor and washed windows, and now she was hanging the paintings that had been leaning against the wall. She hung the last one and stepped back, brushing her hair out of her face. "Okay," she said, "I'll take a break."

"Great," Mr. O'Halloran said. "Want some lunch?"

"Well—sure," Holly said uncertainly.

She was afraid Mr. O'Halloran would do something humiliating, such as give her five dollars and tell her to run along to the coffee shop, but he smiled and said, "I have some stuff in the fridge in back." He hesitated. "You know, we should eat up here, now that it's so clean and everything."

Holly looked around doubtfully. "Where?"

"Here, on the floor. It'll be like a picnic," Mr. O'Halloran said. "I'll be right back."

He bounded into the back room.

Holly rubbed her arms, which hurt from all the lifting. She glanced down at herself and laughed. She had worn black leggings and a black turtleneck, thinking that this would make her look artistic in some way. Now the leggings were covered with lint and sawdust, and the turtleneck had a big smear of rust on it from one of the pipe lengths she had moved. She brushed her fingers over her face lightly, hoping that she was removing dust instead of leaving it. She wanted to look at herself in a mirror, but before she could slip off to the bathroom, Mr. O'Halloran was back, carrying a large paper bag.

They settled down on the carpet in a patch of afternoon sunlight. Mr. O'Halloran opened the bag and spread out their lunch: two hard-boiled eggs (complete with salt in a twist of wax paper), a tomato-and-mozzarella sandwich, an apple, a small bag of pecans, and a bottle of Perrier.

"I can't eat your lunch," Holly protested.

"Don't be silly," Mr. O'Halloran said. "There's plenty for two."

So Holly took a hard-boiled egg and half the mozzarella sandwich. She wondered if Mr. O'Halloran's wife had packed his lunch.

"I can't believe everything you've done today," he commented, looking around. "You're a miracle worker."

Holly smiled, pleased. "All I did was a little fall cleaning," she said.

"Are you kidding? This is great," Mr. O'Halloran said, gesturing at his newly uncluttered gallery. "This is fantastic. This is a major artistic achievement."

Holly laughed. "I *cleaned.* I didn't do anything that required even a modicum of artistic ability."

"Speaking of artistic ability, have classes started yet?" Mr. O'Halloran asked.

Holly nodded, swallowing a bite of her sandwich. "I love them. There's this teacher, Isabelle—"

"What about the other students?" Mr. O'Halloran cut in.

"What about them?" Holly asked, a little startled by the interruption.

He smiled. "Have you met anyone, is what I'm asking. Is my wonderful new assistant going to fall in love and quit?"

"I—" Holly paused, flustered. Imagine someone just assuming that she, Holly, would have a serious boyfriend within the first days of classes! Most people, Holly included, were a little cautious about assuming that Holly would *ever* have a serious boyfriend.

"Mr. O'Halloran—Alan—" She paused again. She was supposed to call him Alan, but she didn't feel comfortable with it, so she tried never to address him directly. "You'll see plenty of me," she said lamely. "I don't think I'll have a boyfriend anytime soon."

"You can't be serious," Mr. O'Halloran said, smiling at her playfully.

"I am," Holly said. "I—" She faltered. What was she going to say? *Boys don't like me?*

"You're going to have a boyfriend in five seconds," Mr. O'Halloran predicted. "A beautiful girl like you? Are you crazy?"

Holly shook her head, blushing. *A beautiful girl like you . . .* Like her? Like Holly Wright?

Mr. O'Halloran took a sharp knife and peeled the skin off the apple in one long, unbroken ribbon.

"Hey, that's very impressive," Holly told him. "I don't know any party tricks like that. If I ever have children, they won't respect me."

Mr. O'Halloran looked amused. "Is this the kind of thing that children respect?"

"Oh, yes," Holly said. "My father could wiggle his ears, and for years I thought that was his only redeeming quality."

He laughed. "Do you want children, Holly?"

She nodded. "I like babies."

"Me too," he said. "But my wife—well, she has other ideas." His eyes were distant.

Holly was silent, not knowing what to say.

Mr. O'Halloran focused on her and smiled. "But enough about my dismal private life," he said lightly.

"Oh, is it really dismal?" Holly blurted out. She was used to her own private life being dismal, but the idea that other people's lives were unfulfilling took her by surprise, especially when it concerned someone as self-assured as Mr. O'Halloran seemed to be.

Her boss looked faintly amused. "It's not the end of the world, Holly," he said. "Lots of people have unhappy marriages. My wife doesn't like or understand this business. You get married too soon and— Well, it's a long story."

He crushed the paper bag and swept the crumbs they'd dropped into his hand. He looked around the gallery. "I still can't believe how different it looks," he said. "So sunny and open."

Holly followed his glance. The gallery did look cheerier and less cluttered. And she was glad she'd washed the windows. It made the place so much brighter, she thought.

She and Mr. O'Halloran sat on the carpet a moment longer. The sun streamed through the clean windows and sparkled on the gold of Mr. O'Halloran's wedding band.

At one o'clock that day, Emily saw a sight that made the bottom of her heart drop out.

She was walking home from campus, strolling through the autumn sunshine, feeling . . . well, feeling very *collegiate*, when she saw a small cluster of people gathered at the top of the hill that led to Folsom Avenue.

She was just making her way to the front of the group when she heard someone scream, "Go, Mac!"

She saw the familiar figure of Mac, sitting cross-legged on a skateboard as though it were a toboggan, pushing with his hands to get started down the hill.

Emily wondered briefly why the sight of Mac flying down a hill in this haphazard fashion would draw a crowd. Why, she'd heard him practicing jumps in the attic the night before, and that seemed a lot more dangerous.

"He's crazy," said the guy standing next to Emily.

"Why do you say that?" Emily asked, still half-watching Mac, who was picking up speed.

The guy pointed. "There's a stop sign at the bottom of the hill," he said.

Emily stared, her eyes widening. There *was* a stop sign at the bottom of the hill, and beyond it, on Folsom Avenue, four lanes of traffic sped merrily by. How was Mac going to stop in time while sitting cross-legged on a skateboard?

"Mac," she whispered. She clutched the sleeve of the guy next to her. "He's going to be killed!" she said hoarsely.

"No, he does this once or twice a year," the guy said. He sounded impressed and wistful.

"He can't *stop,*" Emily said.

"Well, I know," the guy said, a trifle impatiently. "That's what makes it so exciting."

Emily dropped his sleeve and took a few steps forward. Mac was almost to the bottom of the hill now, the skateboard moving nearly as fast as the traffic, Mac's blond hair streaming out behind him.

Emily dropped her books and began running. She flew down the hill, her loafers clunking against the asphalt.

She was less than halfway down when Mac crossed the first lane of traffic. A truck honked, but Mac sailed in front of it. Then the truck sped by, blocking Emily's view.

Her heart was knocking like a fist. She reached the bottom of the hill and plunged into the traffic herself. Cars honked and tires screeched. She didn't hear. She crossed the traffic heedlessly, putting herself in far more danger than Mac had just done. She reached the other side, terrified as she looked for the sight of Mac's crushed and mangled body.

Instead she saw him only a few feet away from her, standing up now, turning lazy circles on his skateboard.

"Mac!" she screamed.

He looked up and smiled. He skated over to her. "Hello—hey!" he protested as she put her hands against his chest and shoved. She pushed him again, and he fell off the skateboard and onto someone's lawn.

"How could you?" she cried. "That was so stupid, so reckless!"

"I saw the way you crossed the street," Mac said mildly from the grass. "Talk about reckless."

"I was trying to save your worthless life!" Emily shouted. Suddenly she burst into tears. "How could you?" she asked again.

Instantly Mac was on his feet next to her. "Don't cry, Emily," he said quietly, putting his arm around her. "I'm okay, really."

"I *know* that," she said, sniffling and trying to push him away, but Mac only put his other arm around her. She rested her head against his shoulder for a second. "I just can't believe you would do that to me."

Mac laughed. "I didn't know you were there," he said. "Plus you've only known me for two days."

"Well, that doesn't mean I want to see you killed in front of my eyes!" Emily said, stepping away from him. She looked at him accusingly, but his hazel eyes were as kind and serious as always. She looked away, confused.

She wiped her eyes with the heel of her hand and looked back up the hill.

"I think the least you can do is go up there and get my books," she said. "I'll see you back at the house."

And she began walking, limping slightly and running her fingers through her tumbled hair.

Paris sat on the lawn outside the student union—the same spot where she and Michael had spoken two days before—and waited for him. She thought the chances were about fifty-fifty that he would show.

She remembered washing dishes with him, holding hands under the suds. And then he'd knocked on her door. She had been in bed, reading with a penlight just in case he knocked. She didn't want things to move too quickly.

He was really very sweet, she thought, although sweet had never counted for very much in Paris's opinion. But Michael had many qualities that did count for a lot: handsomeness, intelligence, sophistication.

And Paris sensed a desperation about Michael that she couldn't put her finger on. He seemed confident, but there was something about him that made her wonder if he was faking it, just a little bit.

Paris turned this thought over in her mind. Possibly he was worried about keeping his grades up. Possibly it was something else. It was the desperation she perceived in him that attracted Paris. She wanted an ally in the house, and she figured it might as well be this handsome, handsome guy.

Suddenly she saw Michael, and she smiled her prettiest smile. He looked a little tired—had he been awake tossing and turning and thinking of her? But he was, as always, impeccably dressed in khakis, a white shirt, and a navy blazer. He was tall, and he carried himself as though he were even taller. Paris held his gaze as he walked toward her.

He sat down next to her on the lawn. "Hi," he said.

"Hello." She leaned forward. "Have a rough morning?"

He ran a hand through his hair. "Yeah, you could say that. I wondered if you'd be here."

"Well, I thought this could be our routine—if that's okay with you," Paris said.

"I'd like that," Michael said, smiling.

Paris found herself staring at his laugh lines. *How does someone get laugh lines when they're only nineteen?* she thought, surprised at, and irritated with, herself for letting those small lines tug at her heart.

She cleared her throat. "Well, good," she said uncertainly. "Are you hungry? Do you want to go inside to the cafeteria?"

Michael shook his head. He leaned over and took her hand. "I only have a couple of minutes," he said. "I think I'd rather just sit here with you—if that's okay with you." His voice was very gently mocking.

Paris smiled. "Okay," she said. After a moment she frowned a little bit and said, "Do you think Emily saw us talking the other day? She looked a little suspicious during dinner."

Michael shrugged. "She could have, I suppose." He waved the air dismissively, brushing the subject away. "Hey, I have some gossip for you."

"What?" Paris said, smiling slyly.

"Remember when Dane left the dinner table, saying that someone was coming over?"

"Yeah."

"Well, Emily went down to his room—for Lord knows what reason; that's probably an even more scandalous story—and do you know what she found?"

"Tell me," Paris said encouragingly, hoping for the worst.

"Dane and this girl he didn't even *know* in some sort of freaky make-out session."

"Oh," Paris said.

"You sound disappointed."

"Well, I thought maybe Emily walked in on Dane as he was getting out of the shower or something."

"Hey, hey, hey," Michael said mildly. "We're talking about my sister here. Try not to gross me out."

"Sorry," Paris said. "Who told you this? Emily?"

"Sure," Michael said. "Who else? Dane?"

"I just wondered how close you and Emily were."

Michael looked thoughtful. "Very close, I think. I guess we're lucky."

"Well, that depends," Paris said. "I wish I could be not close to my family. I wish I could be far away from my family. I wish—" She stopped suddenly.

"What?" Michael said, watching her. "What were you going to say?"

"Nothing," Paris said quickly. "Listen, I went to my botany class this morning, and we have to go out and collect nightshade, if you can believe it. Do you want to come with me? Tonight?"

His eyes flashed briefly. "Sure."

"Good," Paris said. She paused, thinking. "We'll have to leave separately. Why don't we meet by the library at nine o'clock?"

"Okay." Michael glanced at his watch and then stood up reluctantly. "I have to run."

"Good-bye," said Paris, thinking that now that Michael was no longer holding her hand, she felt much more in control of the situation. Which was how she liked it.

The mail arrived just as Holly was getting ready to leave the O'Halloran Showcase.

"Hey, look at this," Mr. O'Halloran said, opening a large pale blue envelope.

"What is it?" Holly asked, pulling on her jacket. Her arms and back ached, and she felt gritty from having touched so many grimy boxes.

"It's an invitation to a fund-raiser for the Art Center," Mr. O'Halloran said. "At a very fancy restaurant. Would you like to go?"

Holly looked at the invitation doubtfully. "Don't you want to go?" she said.

He laughed. "I meant, do you want to go with me?"

Holly bit her lip. "Would that be okay? I mean, isn't that invitation for you?" *You and your wife,* is what she thought.

"Well, I think it would be okay if I brought my lovely assistant," Mr. O'Halloran said.

Lovely, Holly thought. *He's talking about me.* Suddenly she felt like Emily. Wasn't that the way men had talked to Emily since she was ten years old?

Besides, maybe his wife wouldn't go to a fund-raiser, since she didn't like the gallery, she reasoned. She looked at Mr. O'Halloran, trying not to beam. "I'd love to go," she said.

"Good," he said. "It's tomorrow night, and it's formal."

"That's no problem," said Holly, who had owned one dress in her life. It was pink with a Peter Pan collar and had been her favorite dress when she was five years old.

He smiled. "I'll look forward to it," he said. "Why don't you take tomorrow off anyway?"

Holly shook her head. "No, I want to come in and work on the jewelry displays."

"The jewelry displays?" he repeated, as though he'd never noticed them before.

"Well, yes, I was going to clean up that whole area a bit," she said, gesturing toward the wall with the glass cases.

A strange expression flickered across Mr. O'Halloran's face, but he only said kindly, "No, Holly, you've worked hard enough today. Take a day to recover, and tomorrow night we'll go to this thing, then get back to work. Okay?"

"Okay," Holly relented.

She said good-bye and wandered out into the late afternoon warmth. She thought of the fund-raiser, and suddenly she wasn't tired or achy anymore. Something formal! She finally had an excuse to buy something formal. She thought of all the times she'd helped Emily shop for prom dresses or homecoming dresses or Spring Fling dresses. Finally it was her turn, Holly's turn.

She walked up the street, looking at the window displays. She stepped into a few shops, but nothing appealed to her. She was on the brink of going home and asking Paris or someone where to go

when she saw a cream-colored suit on a mannequin in a shop window.

The suit jacket was sleeveless and belted, the
pants were long and flowing. The mannequin wore
a small choker of pearls at her throat. It was the
perfect outfit, Holly thought. She didn't think
dresses were really her style, anyway. Suddenly,
more than anything, she wanted to know what Mr.
O'Halloran would think of her in that suit. He was
married, true, but he could still notice whether
Holly was pretty or not. The thought gave her a
small thrill.

She went into the store and bought the exact
outfit the mannequin was wearing: suit, necklace,
earrings, shoes, and all.

Chapter 8

MICHAEL FOLLOWED PARIS through the woods, watching the glow of her white T-shirt. He felt pretty good. He had a small metal flask in his pocket, containing some more of his Scotch-and-milk mixture. He took a drink. It was helping his hangover immensely.

"Hey, not that I'm complaining," he called to Paris. "But is it strictly necessary to look for nightshade at night?"

"I suppose not," Paris said, "but we had the assignment, and the weather is so nice, I thought we could just take a walk in the woods together."

"Well, except that we're not walking *together*," Michael pointed out. He took another drink from his flask. "I'm trailing behind you like a Japanese wife from the 1200's."

"Like a what?"

He tried to think clearly. "A Japanese wife. From the 1200's. Or something. Weren't they trained to walk several steps behind their husbands?"

"Oh, sorry," Paris said sheepishly. She stopped and waited for him to catch up to her. "Help me look," she said. "I have to examine any plants with purple flowers."

"Nightshade is poisonous," Michael said darkly.

"Only belladonna," Paris said. "And perhaps a few others."

"Well, what kind of assignment is that?" Michael said. He was feeling jolly. "Tonight you have to find some belladonna, and the follow-up assignment is that you have to kill someone with it?"

"You are being so *weird*," Paris said, exasperated.

"I'm tired of looking," Michael said. "Because I can't see anything. We don't even have a flash-light." He glanced down at her. "I can see you, though."

"Well, thanks," Paris said wryly. "I wouldn't want you to forget who you're here with."

"Not a chance," Michael said. He tucked a strand of her hair behind her ear very gently. "I have a great idea," he said. "Let's have a drink."

Holly looked at herself in the mirror and then at Emily. "Are you sure?" she said anxiously. "You don't think I look like a hopeful bride?"

Emily laughed. "No, Holly, I think that suit is perfect," she said. She looked at her with curiosity. "I can't believe you're dating your boss."

"It's not a date," Holly protested.

"What do you mean, it's not a date?" Emily asked. "He asked you out, you bought a new out-fit. Are you going to work tomorrow?"

Holly looked at her quizzically. "No, why?"

"I knew it," Emily said. "You're going to stay home, take a bubble bath, paint your toenails—"

"Shut *up,*" Holly said, throwing one of her new cream-colored pumps at Emily. "It's not a date. He's married."

"He's married?" Emily practically shrieked. "Then why is he taking you and not his wife?"

Holly frowned. "His wife isn't interested in the business, I gather." She shrugged. "But it's not a date, believe me. I mean, was it a date earlier when Dane drove you to the grocery store?"

Emily wrinkled her nose. "*Not,*" she said firmly. "Talk about irritating. He wanted to play this idiotic game with the radio the whole time."

Holly stretched out on the bed next to her. "What kind of game?"

Emily rolled her eyes. "Okay, listen to this. Dane would say something like, 'The next song we hear describes Emily's sex life,' and then he would hit one of the buttons and make a lot of jokes about whatever song came on."

"And what song was it?"

Emily hesitated. "'Sister Christian.'"

Holly laughed. "You're kidding!"

"Hey, you're as bad as he is," Emily said. "I finally distracted him by getting him to play another game where he told me the title and artist of every song after hearing only ten seconds. He was pretty good at it, I'll give him that."

"Why do you let him bother you so much?" Holly asked.

"I don't *let* him," Emily said. "He just *does.*"

Holly was silent. She was thinking about how passionate Emily was about every little thing, about how she invariably cried when talking about air pollution. Holly thought it might not be a bad idea for Emily to go out with someone like Dane, who didn't take anything seriously. Or maybe someone like Mac, who was so laid back. But Holly? Who was the right guy for her? Someone mature and considerate, she thought. Someone like Mr. O'Halloran?

"What are you thinking, doll?" Emily asked. "You look almost sly."

"Nothing," Holly said. She rolled over and buried her face in her pillow. "Nothing at all," she said, her voice muffled, her face flushed and hot.

Dane padded up the stairs in his bare feet. He had been practicing in the basement for hours, and now he wanted to unwind and talk to Emily. He knew that she probably had no interest in talking to him, but that didn't really bother him.

The door to her room was open, but she wasn't inside. The bathroom door opened behind him, and Holly came out. "Hello, Dane," she said.

"Hey, you look fantastic," he said. She was wearing some kind of soft off-white suit, which showed her small waist and beautiful brown arms.

Holly blushed. "Thanks," she said.

"I mean it," Dane said again. "Fantastic." He had noticed that both Emily and Michael treated Holly like their much younger sister, a teeny-bopper who could only stay at home and dream about boys and dates and first kisses.

I'll bet she was plain for most of high school, Dane thought. *And now she's turned gorgeous, but they only see what they've always seen.*

"Look, do you know where Emily is?" he asked.

Holly looked surprised. "She's not in her room?"

Dane shook his head. "I guess she must have gone down to the kitchen or something," he said. "I'll take a look. Good night."

"Good night," Holly said, and went into her room.

Dane turned to go back downstairs and then paused thoughtfully at the stairs to Mac's room. Could Emily be up there?

Dane's green eyes narrowed, but then he shrugged. Jealousy was not part of his nature. He bounced back down the stairs, singing "Take Me Out to the Ball Game" deliberately off-key and way too loud.

Emily sat on the sleeping bag in Mac's room. She was thinking that his room looked like the pro shop at a ski resort. Skis and snowboards leaned against the walls, and blown-up trail maps of ski areas covered most of the wall space.

The sleeping bag wasn't especially comfortable, but it was the only choice. The rest of the floor space was devoted to Mac's Rollerblading course, which was marked by bright orange traffic cones. Emily didn't ask how he had gotten them.

Mac was restlessly skating through his slalom course, doing slow turns and spins.

"Aren't you afraid that one of the boards is going to give and you'll fall through the floor and break your neck?" she asked.

"No," Mac said. Then he frowned. "At least, I wasn't a second ago."

Emily laughed. "Sorry."

Mac flashed her a smile. "That's okay. . . . You know, I'm glad you came up here. I thought you were still mad at me after today."

Sighing, Emily curled up on her side on the sleeping bag. "No, I'm not mad at you anymore," she said. "It just upsets me to see people taking crazy chances."

"Why?" Mac skated over and stood next to her. From Emily's position on the floor, he looked twelve feet tall. "Why do you care what other people do?"

Emily frowned. "I don't know. I just do. I always have." She sat up. "Do you hear something?"

Mac listened. "Nope."

"I thought I heard voices," Emily said. "It sounded like Michael. . . ." She shook her head. "Anyway, I'm glad you're okay. I'd better go downstairs. I'm getting sleepy."

"Oh," Mac said, sounding disappointed. He pulled her to her feet, which was impressive considering he was wearing Rollerblades.

"Good night," Emily said, holding out her hand. Suddenly she felt ridiculous. *I must look like I'm from the Chamber of Commerce or something,* she thought.

She dropped her hand before Mac could reach for it and surprised both of them by leaning up and kissing his cheek.

Mac looked at her. "Good night," he said uncertainly.

"Good night," Emily repeated, feeling even more ridiculous than before.

She slipped out of his room and was halfway down the curving staircase before she realized that she had just kissed the most handsome guy she'd ever met. Plus she'd saved his life (or so she would come to think of it years later). Not a bad day, all in all.

Michael and Paris crashed into the banister and burst into laughter. They had shared the contents of Michael's flask and then an old bottle of sweet wine Michael kept in the trunk of his car.

As Michael slipped an arm around her waist, Paris yelped. His fingers were so cold, she could feel them even through her T-shirt. "Shhh," she said, giggling.

"You're telling *me* to be quiet when you're the one who made the noise?" Michael teased, blowing on his fingers to warm them. "Come here."

"Michael, we can't," Paris whispered. "Not here on the stairs. Someone will catch us."

Michael grinned. "So I'll race you to your room."

He chased her up the stairs, stumbling near the top. Paris ran into her room, still giggling loudly. He caught up with her and slipped his arms around her waist from the back.

She leaned her head against his shoulder. "Michael?"

"Yes?" He kissed her neck.

"I don't feel so good."

He looked at her. Perspiration had sprung out on her forehead, and her eyes looked glassy. "Oh, Paris," he said.

"What?" she asked. She took a couple of deep breaths. "Is it hot in here?"

"Come on," said Michael gently, turning her around. "Let's get you to the kitchen and make some coffee. I think you're in for a rough night."

Holly was sitting on the iron bench on the roof and so she had seen Michael and Paris come up the front lawn, stumbling and clutching each other.

I knew it, she thought, but somehow she didn't feel the pang of exile she usually felt when she found out about someone else's relationship.

She pulled the blanket closer around her and stared out at the lights of their neighborhood. Her housemates were still awake—Holly could see the wavering squares of light their windows cast onto the front lawn. Even Dane was awake in the basement, his lava lamp creating a small red glow near the window well.

Holly was thinking about Mr. O'Halloran. Would he come to the house to pick her up the next evening? She would have to wear high heels since she was so short and he was so tall. Would she have to hobble down to the bus stop in her high heels? Well, if he didn't drive her, she would have Michael drop her off.

And what would happen once she and Mr. O'Halloran were at the party? Would he tell her again that she was beautiful? What would she say to him? Holly felt her heart flutter with anxiety and excitement. Just to be safe, she'd better think of a few topics ahead of time.

Holly realized she had been practically unraveling the blanket, she was fidgeting so much. *Will you relax already?* she told herself. *First of all, he's married, even if unhappily. And he probably only flatters you because you work for him and he likes happy employees or something.*

But Holly couldn't relax. She couldn't stop thinking about Mr. O'Halloran. She imagined how happy she'd be if he pulled out her chair for her at dinner the next evening.

She stayed up very late thinking about these things, her breath making faint silvery plumes in the night air. She didn't go inside even after everyone else in the house went to bed, their windows going dark one by one, until even Dane's lava lamp trembled and blinked out.

Chapter 9

PARIS DIDN'T WAKE UP UNTIL FIVE the next afternoon. Her first thought was: *There is hair growing on my tongue.* Her tongue also seemed to be stuck to the roof of her mouth.

She groaned and sat up, which sent a spike of pain through her temple. She winced and rubbed her head carefully.

What on earth happened last night? she thought. Then she remembered. That horrible sweet watermelon wine. She, Paris Newman, was hung over from watermelon wine. She grimaced and swung her legs out of bed.

A note was taped to her door. *Hope you survive. I'll be home to take care of you later. M.* Paris crumpled the note up and dropped it on the floor.

The image in the bathroom mirror was as bad as she'd feared: bleary eyes, stale makeup, blotchy skin. She stepped into the shower.

Ten minutes later she wandered into the kitchen, looking, if not feeling, much better. She wore jeans and a black turtleneck. Her long hair was pulled back into a ponytail, and makeup concealed the dark circles under her eyes. Only the pained, irritable look in her eyes hinted at her hung-over state.

She pulled the orange juice out of the refrigerator and drank straight from the carton. She swallowed, feeling a little better. She wiped her lips with the back of her hand and leaned against the counter.

Idly she reread the house rules, and then something on the refrigerator door caught her eye. The dinner roster. She, Paris, was supposed to make dinner that night.

She felt like throwing the juice carton across the room. Emily and her stupid chores! They were supposed to eat dinner at six, and it was almost five-thirty.

Well, there's only one solution, she decided. She grabbed the yellow pages off the counter and went to work.

Holly dressed slowly and deliberately. She had thought about putting her hair up in some sophisticated twist, but she figured that if she did she'd spend the whole evening trying to keep her head still, so she just brushed it carefully and let it curl naturally. She spent fifteen minutes applying makeup and then decided ruefully that there wasn't a lot more she could do.

She glanced at the clock. Mr. O'Halloran was coming to pick her up in ten minutes. How slowly this day was going! She wandered around her room, not wanting to sit down and wrinkle her suit.

Don't be stupid, Holly told herself. *Your suit's going to get wrinkled in the car anyway.* She had a brief image of riding in the car next to Mr. O'Halloran, him driving, her kneeling stiffly in her seat, not sitting, still valiantly trying to keep her clothes wrinkle-free.

Oh, man. Mr. O'Halloran probably never gave her a thought beyond tax forms or whatever, and here she was, going crazy.

She decided to go downstairs and wait for him. She grabbed her impossibly small cream-colored handbag, which contained only a ten-dollar bill and a tube of lipstick, and opened her bedroom door.

Immediately she heard the sound of angry voices from below.

Paris knew there was going to be trouble the minute she saw the tiny frown between Emily's eyebrows. The frown had appeared as soon as everyone had trooped into the dining room and Emily had seen the table.

Paris thought—modestly or no—that the table looked beautiful, set with mouthwateringly delicious food. Which was no small feat, since it had been arranged by someone who felt as though elves were tapping on her skull with small hammers.

"Please sit down," she said graciously.

"Chinese," Mac said. "Great."

Emily paused. "You didn't cook all this?" she said to Paris, but it wasn't really a question.

Paris shrugged, a gesture which could've meant *What can I say, I'm a great cook* or *Guilty as charged.*

They began eating. There were bowls of sweet-and-sour pork, chicken with peanuts, spicy cabbage, broccoli and snow peas.

"This is great," Dane said. "You're a wonderful cook."

"You don't actually—" Emily began, but Paris cut her off.

"Thank you, Dane," she said smoothly.

"Do you cook French food, too?" Dane asked.

"No, why?"

"Well, I thought you were French, because of your name."

Paris shook her head. "No, I'm not French. I was conceived in Paris, that's how I got my name."

Dane's eyes twinkled. "What are your brothers' and sisters' names?"

A strange look passed over Paris's face. "Nothing exotic," she said softly.

"What restraint," Emily said under her breath.

"Look, at least my parents bothered to *space* their children," Paris responded hotly. "Which is more than I can say for yours."

"Paris," Michael said quietly. There was a warning in his voice.

But Paris ignored it. "Just what is your problem, Emily? You've been giving me dirty looks ever since you sat down to dinner."

Emily's eyes narrowed. "And after you've obviously slaved over a hot stove all day, too."

"So what if I didn't cook dinner?" Paris said, exasperated. "I still arranged for it. I still put it on the table."

"That's not the point," Emily said. "Everyone else cooks when it's his or her turn. You think that just because you have money, you're above that."

"Emily," Michael said pleadingly.

"What?" She turned to him.

"Please, it's not important."

"It is important," Emily said. "If we're all going to live here and learn to get along—"

"Oh, you are so self-righteous," Paris spat out, throwing down her napkin and pushing back her chair. "I can't stand another minute of this. My head is pounding."

Mac and Dane were studying their plates.

"Paris—" Michael said.

"Oh, spare me whatever soothing thing you're going to say," Paris snapped. "It's your fault I feel so rotten, anyway."

Emily's eyes widened. She pushed back her chair, too. "I see," she said. She looked from Paris to Michael. "I see exactly how it is now."

And she too threw down her napkin. She stormed out the front door, while Paris stomped out of the dining room, brushing past Holly, who was standing in the doorway.

Emily huffed across the front lawn, getting angrier with every step. So Michael was responsible for Paris's headache, was he? That meant they had been together the night before. And that made Emily angry on a couple of levels.

First, did Paris's headache mean that they had been drinking together? Emily supposed it did. She knew that Michael drank. She'd seen him at parties in high school, and once in a while she thought she smelled it on his breath. This bothered her, not because she was worried about Michael—he could handle anything, she was sure—but because it would upset their parents no end. Their father had "a problem with alcohol." That's what he told them. He said he was not an alcoholic, but that it was simply better for all concerned if he didn't drink.

It upset her far more that he had been drinking with *Paris*. Oh, how could he! Didn't he see how cold she was? And arrogant? And selfish? Her remarks about Emily still stung. *You're so self-righteous.*

Emily slowed her pace a little. Was she self-righteous? She didn't think so. It was just that they had all agreed to cook dinner, and ordering Chinese food seemed like cheating.

Of course they had *also* all agreed not to date each other. Emily's mind circled back to Michael and Paris. She could kill him! To think of all the snide remarks he'd made over the years about Frank! In her anger, she forgot that she had always secretly felt like cheering when he said mean things about Frank. But at least Frank was a nice person, at least he was kind.

Emily stopped walking, realizing she was back where she had started, in front of the house. She had circled the block, stomping along angrily. She wondered suddenly if some family had looked up from the dinner table and seen her march by with a furious scowl on her face. Maybe the little kid of the family had said, *Daddy, why does that lady look so mad?* and the dad had said—

"Emily?" said a quiet voice.

She jumped and looked up. Mac was sitting in the shadows on the front porch.

She smiled weakly. "Hi, Mac," she said. She sat down next to him.

He had a jacket folded in his lap, and now he shook it out and gave it to her. "I thought you might get cold," he said. "You looked so angry when you left that I thought it might be a while before you calmed down enough to go inside."

"Thanks," Emily said, pulling the jacket around her. "That was very nice of you."

He shrugged. "So Holly just left with some guy," he said after a pause.

"Oh, yeah," Emily said. "Her boss. I forgot she was going out."

Suddenly she wished she hadn't mentioned Holly's boss. Now Mac was going to get all interested and ask her a few thousand questions.

But Mac didn't seem to give another thought to Holly and her boss. "Do you feel better?" he asked gently.

She sighed. "Not really. I can't decide who I'm angrier with, Paris or Michael. I just— I don't know." She looked at him suddenly in the twilight. "Do you think I overreacted?"

Mac stretched, looking absolutely noncommittal. "I think we should go for a bike ride."

"What?"

"I think we should go for a bike ride," he repeated. "It's going to be too cold in a few days. Want to go?"

"Well . . ." Emily hesitated, caught off guard. "Well, first of all, it's dark, and second of all, I don't have a bicycle."

"I have a flashlight tied to the front of my bike," Mac said. "I'll balance you on the handlebars. Come on."

He stood up and held out his hand. Emily touched his fingers briefly as she stood. She followed him around to the back of the house, where he kept his bike locked up.

It was not the sort of bicycle you would expect Mac to ride. It was an elderly, clunky bike with a big basket in front. But Mac had maintained the bike beautifully, and it ran smoothly.

He untied the flashlight from the handlebars and handed it to her. Then he got on the bike, and she climbed into the basket.

"I feel like your pet dog," Emily said as he began pedaling. "Or like Toto in *The Wizard of Oz* when he rides in that basket."

"If you're Toto, that makes me the Wicked Witch of the West," Mac said, panting a little from the effort of pedaling. "Hey, you have to light the way with the flashlight."

"Sorry." Emily adjusted the light. "Hey!" she said as the bike swerved. "This is a little scary."

Mac pedaled faster. "Did anyone ever tell you

you're disaster-oriented?" he said, but his voice was kind. "I lay awake all last night, thinking I could hear the floor giving way."

He swerved the bike again, and Emily shrieked, but her cry ended in laughter. They kept going, in long, lazy, dangerous turns, the bike practically on its side, until they had circled the block many times and Emily's laughter had filled the night air.

Holly could not think up one intelligent thing to say to Mr. O'Halloran on the way to the restaurant. In fact, she couldn't think up one *un*intelligent thing to say to him, either, so she said nothing at all.

He told her she looked nice (actually he said "incredible"), and she smiled gratefully. He told her that the restaurant they were going to was a historic landmark, and she smiled interestedly. He told her that usually these fund-raiser things were really dull and she must let him know if she got bored, and she tried to smile intelligently.

By the time they got to the restaurant and ordered drinks from the bartender, she was thinking that she would spend the entire evening trying to express complex thoughts and feelings through various smiles.

Very gently Mr. O'Halloran took her hand. "Nervous?" he said.

She nodded, her heart starting to thump at his touch.

"Well, there's no need to be," he said. He

squeezed her hand and released it as their drinks arrived.

Holly took a sip of her daiquiri. "There is alcohol in this," she announced. It was her first sentence of the evening.

Mr. O'Halloran laughed. "It walks, it talks, it stands on two feet like a man," he said.

Holly laughed, too. She took another sip of her daiquiri. Mr. O'Halloran watched her. "Don't you drink?"

"Not old enough," Holly said.

"Well, it's okay, they won't be carding at an event like this," he said. He glanced around the room. "See anyone you want to talk to?"

Now this was precisely the kind of thing Holly hated. What was she supposed to say? If she said, *Yeah, I think that guy looks pretty interesting,* she'd sound like a heartless flirt. If she said, *Nope, nobody looks worth bothering with at all,* she'd sound stuck up.

She tried to think what Emily or Paris would do in this situation. Finally she gestured to a stout woman with pearl-framed eyeglasses and said, "I think I'd like to talk to her."

He looked at the stout woman. "Really? Well, I can certainly introduce you. Why do you want to talk to her?"

Holly sighed. "Because—because she looks like my first-grade teacher, which leads me to believe that she's a motherly sort of person," she confessed. "And I think she'll be nice to me."

Mr. O'Halloran burst out laughing. He put his arm around Holly. "Come on," he said. "Let's go sit in the courtyard." He led her through the back doors of the restaurant to a small terrace with olive trees and stone benches. A tiny patch of sky showed above their heads.

"Oh, this is nice," Holly said.

"I thought you'd like to get outside for a bit," Mr. O'Halloran said, smiling. "These parties can be pretty deadly."

They sat down on a bench. Holly looked back into the restaurant and did a double take. Someone who looked like Michael had just disappeared into the crowd at the bar. But that was ridiculous. What would Michael be doing here?

Mr. O'Halloran shrugged out of his suit jacket and draped it around her shoulders.

"Oh, I'm okay," Holly protested, even though she'd actually been chilly. She felt awkward about accepting his jacket, as though she were making a pass at him.

"Don't be silly," he said. "It's cool out here." He stretched out his long legs and examined the tips of his shoes. "Holly, I have a confession to make."

"You do?" This was interesting; usually it was Holly who had the confessing to do. *Sorry, I wasn't listening. Sorry, I can't remember.*

"Yes, I—" Mr. O'Halloran hesitated. "Actually a couple of confessions. First of all, I know you've never worked in a gallery before."

Holly's heart sank. "Nancy McCabe?" she whispered.

He nodded. "I called her for a reference, and she kept talking about tips and good memories and chicken wings."

Holly felt her cheeks flame in the darkness. Nancy McCabe must not have understand what she meant by "vague reference."

This is the most embarrassing moment of my life, Holly thought miserably. *All the rest of my life, humiliating things will happen to me, and I'll think, well, at least it's not as bad as that one time . . .*

"So I guess I'm fired," she said quietly.

"What are you talking about?" Mr. O'Halloran asked. "I hired you *after* I called your reference."

"Y-you did?" Holly stammered. She managed to look directly at him for the first time. "Why?"

"Well, that's the confession," he said. He was still examining his shoes. "You turned out to be such a great assistant that I can't believe my luck, but . . ." He glanced up and met her eyes. "I hired you because you were just about the prettiest girl I'd ever seen."

"Oh," Holly breathed. It sounded like a squeak.

They looked at each other for a very long moment, a moment during which Holly's senses seemed totally numb. Then suddenly everything was back, and better than before: the music from inside sounded sweeter, the leaves on the trees were more sharply defined, the night air was cooler and more fragrant. It seemed, to Holly, like a scene from a movie, directed by someone with melodramatic but beautiful taste.

Chapter 10

"ANOTHER GIN AND TONIC?" THE bartender asked.

Michael nodded. The bartender refilled his drink. Michael took a long, appreciative swallow. He had needed a drink so much after that dinner scene, but his Scotch-and-milk thermos was empty, and he and Paris had polished off his last-resort watermelon wine.

So he'd put on his best suit and tie and checked the newspaper for benefits or fund-raisers. He knew from experience that they rarely carded at formal functions and that if he sat at the bar and looked dignified and aloof, nobody ever asked him why he was there. Sometimes, like that night, he even got the drinks for free.

Michael took another long drink of gin. The knot in his stomach was slowly dissolving. That was the beauty of alcohol, he thought. It was a sure-fire cure; it always worked one hundred percent.

As the alcohol relaxed him he thought about Paris. Had it been a mistake to drink with her?

Maybe, but he hadn't realized how drunk she was. She obviously blamed him for her hangover, which must have been fierce to make her so callous to Emily.

And what was he going to do about Emily? She was furious, and, Michael knew, likely to get more furious. Once Emily felt betrayed, she didn't get over it easily.

He finished his gin and considered ordering a third one. He would love another drink—or a bunch of other drinks—but at these fund-raisers they sometimes got suspicious after a few rounds. Besides, he had to go home in a relatively alert condition in case Paris, Emily, or both were lying in wait to argue with him.

So reluctantly he said good-bye to the bartender and stood up. At least he'd had two drinks. That helped a little.

Paris paced her room nervously, wearing only a short black nightgown, her long blond hair swinging. She had crept down to the kitchen and eaten a big plate of leftover Chinese food, and now she felt much better. If only someone had told her that eating would help her hangover! Then perhaps she wouldn't have lost her temper.

Her bare feet padded restlessly on the wooden floor. Where was Michael? She wandered out to the landing and peered over the railing down the stairs. She had been doing this all night and had observed all sorts of commotion: Mac and Emily, first coming in, then going back out, then home again later, whispering; Dane and his idiotic band pals yukking it up, invading the kitchen, wearing pots and pans and colanders as helmets and staging gladiator fights; Holly drifting up the stairs, her eyes as dreamy as chocolate mousse.

But no Michael. Paris paced back into her room. What if he was mad at her for letting it slip that they'd been out the night before? What if he was mad at her for snapping at his beloved sister? What if he came home and had a long talk with Emily and then didn't—

She heard footsteps on the stairs and ran back to the landing, leaning over the railing, her hair falling over her shoulders.

"Michael?"

He was coming up the stairs slowly, tiredly. He looked up at her.

"Hello, Paris."

She brushed the hair off her face and stared at him nervously, her blue eyes large and anxious. "Oh, Michael," she whispered. She scampered around the railing and down a few steps, then stopped, the short black nightgown stirring around her thighs. Her legs were the color of honey.

"I'm so sorry about the way I acted, the things I said to you and to Emily," she said. "Especially to Emily."

Of course, I should be giving this apology to Emily, but that's not the point, she thought. *It's you that I hope it works on.*

Michael sighed. "It's okay, Paris," he said.

"It is?" Paris asked. "Is it really? You're not just saying that?"

He smiled faintly. "I'm not just saying that. It really is."

For a moment neither of them said anything. Paris twisted the ends of her hair. "Then why are you standing so far away from me?" she asked.

Michael looked at her for a moment, then his eyes twinkled, and he bounded up the steps separating them and grabbed her around the waist. The fabric of the black nightgown flowed over his fingers as he caressed her. Paris laughed and threw her arms around his neck, covering his face with kisses until she felt the laugh lines around his eyes underneath her lips and knew she was forgiven.

While she brushed her teeth, Emily rehearsed what she would say to Michael. She would try to be cool and nonjudgmental, like Mac.

She stared at her reflection in the bathroom mirror and tried to erase the vertical line that sometimes formed between her eyebrows. She had read in a book once that it was called the "I-want line," and that bothered her tremendously.

Okay. She would say, *Michael, I just want to apologize for my behavior tonight. It was inexcusable.*

There. That was perfect. Simple, to the point. She wouldn't justify it further than that. She wouldn't say that she still resented the fact that Paris had ordered Chinese food, or that she thought Michael would have better taste than to fall for the Ice Queen. She would say she was sorry and that was that. That's what Mac would do. The right thing.

She sighed. It wasn't what she, Emily, would naturally do, though. She wanted to hash everything out in the most disorganized and excited of ways, as she had at the house meeting. But, she reminded herself, maybe her way wasn't the best way. She could learn to change.

Realizing that she had probably brushed the enamel off her teeth by now, Emily stopped brushing and rinsed. She checked the mirror once more for the I-want line and padded down the stairs to Michael's room.

His door was shut, but there was a very faint glow underneath, as though he had the desk light on.

Emily knocked. No answer.

She knocked again and was on the point of calling his name when she heard a noise, as soft as a cat's step, but as distinctive as popcorn. A giggle.

And then a voice saying, "Shhh."

Emily's temper flared, a sudden furious burst. It was a wonder that, in that moment, she didn't just throw open the door and storm in. She stood, hurt, horrified, then spun on her heel and marched back up the stairs to her room, the I-want line firmly in place.

They were not all together again until the next night at dinner. It was Mac's night to cook, and to everyone's surprise, he had created a feast. Pot roast with new potatoes and carrots sat on a platter in the middle of the table. Hot rolls steamed in a basket, and there was a bowl of gravy, too. Mac had even unearthed cloth napkins.

Unfortunately, his delicious dinner was for the most part unappreciated. Michael and Paris sat on one side of the table, sharing long, slow smiles between bites of pot roast. Emily sat across from them, with Mac at her side. Her spine was straight and she kept her chin held high. She refused to look at Michael. Holly sat at one end of the table, apparently watching a movie none of the rest of them could see. Her eyelids fluttered from time to time, and occasionally her lips moved silently. She was absently eating a roll, completely unaware of any tension at the table. Dane was sitting at the other end of the table, watching everybody and thinking that he shouldn't spend so much time in the basement because more interesting things were obviously afoot.

He was watching Holly, privately betting that she would accidentally bite her tongue any minute now and wondering if he would be able to tell from her face when she did, when Emily turned to Mac and said with deliberate sweetness, "This is a wonderful meal, Mac. You must've worked very hard."

Mac looked uncomfortable for a moment, but then his usual ease returned. "We, um, we had a housekeeper when I was growing up," he said. "It was sort of like living in a fancy restaurant."

"I worked at Burger King one summer," Dane said in a conversational tone. Emily and Mac looked at him blankly. "Well, I thought it was sort of on the same subject," he said defensively.

Emily sighed irritably. "The same subject as what?"

"Well, food in general."

"We weren't talking about food in general," Emily said. "We were talking about Mac's cooking experience, because he made such a wonderful dinner. We aren't interested in your summer at Burger King."

"Why not?" Dane said. "I tell you, it would be far from the most boring conversation we've ever had. In fact, the first night you held us all spellbound while you debated whether not or we should vacuum every third day or—"

"Okay," Emily said hastily. "Tell us your story."

"Well, I don't know," Dane said thoughtfully. "It's had a lot of buildup now, and it's not actually that great a story."

"I'd like to hear it," Holly said, surprising everyone.

Emily turned to her. "You would?"

"Yes," Holly said softly. "Dane's stories aren't like anyone else's."

"I know," Emily said. "They seldom have a point. But go ahead."

"Okay," Dane said. "I worked the night shift at Burger King, and at the end of the summer the manager called us all into his office and said, 'I think you should know that I bugged the break room, and here is a tape of all the mean things you said about me,' and he played the tape."

Even Paris and Michael were listening. "What was on the tape?" Paris asked.

"Oh, the usual, I think. I can't really remember,"

Dane said. "He'd spliced it together very professionally, though."

"If you can't even remember what was on the tape, what was the point of that story?" Emily asked.

"The point," Dane repeated. "The point is that the manager had listened to God knows how many hours of our break-room talk in order to get the parts where we said mean things about him. Can you imagine what his life was like for him to want to do that?" He twisted his lips thoughtfully. "Well, maybe you can, Emily. You're very interested in what other people think."

He pushed back his chair. "Come on, Holly, it's our turn to do the dishes."

"Hey, far be it from me to criticize you," Dane said to Holly, "but you've washed that glass more thoroughly than—than I don't know what. More thoroughly than my sister washed her hair before her senior prom."

Holly laughed and handed him the glass to rinse. "How thoroughly did your sister wash her hair?"

"Oh, man," Dane said. "It was incredible. First she washed it with an egg, then she washed it with beer, and I think maybe with some milk, too. I remember because I was thinking that her hair would probably end up smelling like a casserole or something. Plus she washed it in the kitchen sink, which seemed appropriate. And in the end it looked basically the same as it looked every single day."

Holly smiled and handed him another glass. "That's why I like your stories," she said softly.

"Why?"

She frowned as she considered. "Because they don't have punch lines, I guess," she said finally. "I don't like stories with punch lines because I'm usually not paying that much attention, and so I don't get it. But I don't have to pay attention to your stories."

"Gee, thanks," Dane said. "I don't think I could ask for a higher compliment." He looked thoughtful. "Although you do at least like my stories, as opposed to Emily."

Holly glanced at him. "Why do you always give Emily such a hard time?" she asked cautiously.

"Because I'm crazy about her," Dane said instantly.

"Oh," Holly said. She washed a plate about five times, not realizing what she was doing. She thought about all the boys who had told her this over the years. They were beyond number, these boys who had looked deep into her eyes and confessed their love for Emily. Usually Holly felt a little bit like crying when this happened, but it was different this time. This time she had the memory of Mr. O'Halloran (she still thought of him that way) telling her she took his breath away.

"You know," Holly said slowly, "if you wanted me to, I could maybe arrange for you two to be alone."

"You would do that?" Dane asked.

"Well, sure," Holly said. Why not? Why

shouldn't Emily be as happy with Dane as Holly hoped she was going to be with Mr. O'Halloran?

Dane splashed the rinse water reflectively. "I could make her dinner," he said softly. "On Saturday, just the two of us. I'd make a dinner just as good as Mac's."

"I'll see what I can do," Holly said. She stared out the window, lost in thought. Despite Dane's earlier plea, she was still washing each dish a couple of times without thinking about it. But then Holly did most things slowly and dreamily. Once a man had come up to her in a restaurant and told her that he was on a diet and she was eating her meal so slowly that it was torturing him.

But Dane was no longer paying attention. He was lost in thoughts of his own.

Chapter 11

EMILY CAME HOME AT NOON AND entered the house cautiously. She didn't especially feel like running into anyone—Michael, Paris, Dane, even Holly, who only wanted to talk about Mr. O'Halloran.

Emily sighed. She knew she was being unfair to Holly. Once in high school when Emily had been chattering on about some boy, Holly had told her she was suffering from the But-Bob-Doesn't-Like-Peas Syndrome. That, Holly said, was when you fell in love with someone and felt compelled to bore all your friends with every little detail about the loved one until it became so all-consuming that one night at dinner your mother said, *Why aren't you eating your peas, dear?* and you said, *But Bob doesn't like peas!* Hence the name.

So anyway, Emily knew that she had probably put Holly through enough of that sort of thing that she ought to be able to put up with a few details about Mr. O'Halloran. But Emily *did* have more than a couple of doubts about Mr. O'Halloran. For instance, if he was so unhappily married, why didn't he get divorced?

Still, she resolved, as soon as Holly got home, Emily would get her alone and *ask* her for boring details about Mr. O'Halloran. *Like maybe what his first name is,* she thought.

Emily went into the kitchen and began making herself a sandwich. She hadn't meant to shut Holly out; it was just that she was still so upset about Paris and Michael.

She had replayed the giggle and the whispered hushing a million times in her head, trying to come up with a scenario that didn't include Paris and Michael being in bed together.

Paris and Michael are listening to Spanish-language tapes on Michael's stereo. Paris giggles at something, and Michael says, "Shhh, I'm trying to conjugate this verb."

Emily shook her head. Neither one was even taking a Spanish class. She tried another one.

Michael has lost one of his contact lenses, and they're crawling around looking for it. Paris starts to feel foolish and giggles. Michael says, "Shhh, I'm concentrating."

Emily rolled her eyes. She was really grasping at straws. You didn't have to be quiet to find a contact lens. Plus they would've answered the door. She racked her brain for yet another one.

Paris and Michael are in bed together. They hear chucklehead Emily knocking at the door. They know she has come to apologize. Paris finds this so pathetic she giggles. "Shhh," Michael says, "she'll hear you."

Never Fall in Love

Now, that had the ring of truth to it, didn't it? Emily rubbed her temple. How had things gone so terribly wrong in this house in only a few days? She finished making her turkey sandwich and was about to take a bite when she heard soft guitar chords from the basement. Dane was home.

Emily felt a twinge of shame as Dane's words to her at the dinner table the night before leaped into her mind. *You care so much about other people's lives, Emily.* Insinuating that she didn't have enough in her own life. Well, how could she blame him for thinking that when she had trouble getting along with practically half the household?

Quickly, before she could change her mind, Emily cut her sandwich in half, put it on a plate, and went cautiously down the basement stairs.

Dane was lounging in a beanbag chair in the soft glow of his lava lamp, playing a song on the guitar that Emily didn't recognize. He evidently was not playing it to his satisfaction, because he kept shaking his head and playing the same part over and over.

She knocked on the wall softly, and Dane looked up.

"Hey," he said, smiling.

"Hi. I heard you practicing," she said awkwardly, "and I thought you might like something to eat."

"Gosh, thanks, Emily," Dane said, putting his guitar aside and standing up. "Come on in."

She handed him the sandwich and sat down tentatively on the other beanbag chair.

"Wow, this is great," Dane said, biting into the sandwich.

"You're welcome," Emily said.

"Plus I'm really glad that you cut the sandwich in half diagonally," Dane said.

Emily frowned slightly. "Are you making fun of me?"

Dane looked surprised. "Making fun of you?" he repeated. "Of course not. Believe me, diagonally cut sandwiches are much better."

She crossed her arms. "Why?"

He looked thoughtful. "Because you've got two triangles," he said at last. "And then if it's a thick sandwich, you at least have a sort of narrow starting point."

"Oh," Emily said uncertainly.

"Because sometimes you have a really thick sandwich and someone cuts it in half the other way, you know, so you just have two rectangles," Dane continued. "And that doesn't give you any starting point at all, so why bother?"

Emily gave him a small smile, and, since she could think of nothing more to say about sandwiches, decided to change the subject. "Did you really start playing the guitar because your mother wouldn't let you play the harmonica?"

Dane laughed. "No, you were right about that not being a true story," he said.

"So . . . how *did* you start?"

Dane took another bite of his sandwich. "My parents got divorced when I was fifteen," he said. "My sister and I went to this therapist to learn how to deal with it, and the therapist told us that our dad felt really guilty, and any present we asked him for, he would probably give us. One of the things I asked for was a guitar."

"That's horrible," Emily said.

"Why is it horrible?"

"Well . . ." She had trouble thinking. "You were exploiting his guilt."

Dane laughed. "You are a piece of work," he said.

"What do you mean?"

"I would think that any normal person would want to know what my sister asked for, instead of trying to psychoanalyze the whole thing."

Emily stood up. "I guess I'm not a normal person," she said shortly.

"Yeah, well, neither am I," Dane said mildly. "That's why we'd make a good pair."

"We'd *what?*"

"You heard me," Dane said.

"You are unbelievable," Emily said. "Here I make this nice gesture, and you—"

"Hey, I appreciated the gesture," Dane protested. "Listen, sit down."

"No, thanks," Emily said, moving toward the door.

"My sister asked for a nose job," Dane told her. "Don't you want to know whether she got it or not?"

Emily turned around. "No. Believe it or not, I can live without that information," she said.

"Yeah, well, my hat's off to you," Dane said, still chewing. "A good exit line is hard to beat."

• • •

Michael and Paris skipped their afternoon classes and went to the library, where they camped out on a couch in the reading room, nudging each other's feet and idly reading the morning paper.

Paris had smuggled a cup of coffee into the reading room in her backpack, and now she took it out.

She looked at Michael and smiled. "How are you doing today?"

He smiled back. "I'm fine—very fine—after last night." He was actually a little hung over, but that would pass.

Paris blew on her coffee to cool it and then took a sip. "Listen, there's something I want to ask you."

"There's something I want to ask you, too," Michael said.

"Okay, you first."

Michael looked at her intently. "It's about Emily."

"Uh-uh," Paris said immediately. "No way am I going to apologize."

He laughed. "How do you know that's what I'm going to ask?"

"Isn't it?"

"Well, yes."

Paris took another sip of coffee. "You know, I would apologize to her if she were halfway nice, but she's not even speaking to me. Or looking at me."

"She's angry, Paris."

"Yeah, well, so am I. You know, the more I thought about it, the more unfair I thought it was that she was mad because I ordered dinner instead of cooking it. Nobody said a word when Holly bought that cheesecake."

"I know," said Michael, who had thought of that at the time, but was hoping Paris wouldn't remember. "But to Emily that's different."

"Different how?"

"Because Holly made *most* of the meal—"

"Oh, give me a break," Paris cut in. "So who decides where to draw the line? Last night Mac used rolls he bought from a bakery, too."

"Paris—"

"I'll tell you how it's different," Paris said. "It's different because Emily likes Mac and she likes Holly and she *doesn't* like me. That's how it's different."

Michael sighed. This he couldn't deny. "Paris, can't you just apologize? You said you were sorry last night."

"That was before I knew that she was going to bear a grudge for, like, the rest of her life," Paris said. "She probably wouldn't think it was enough for me just to say that I'm sorry. She'd want me to carry her slippers around in my teeth or something."

"Paris—"

"Anyway, I want to ask you my question now."

"Well, okay," Michael relented.

Paris leaned forward, looking into his eyes. "I was wondering if you want to go away with me this weekend. My dad owns a condo in Estes Park. We could go there and spend a night together, just the two of us." She finished her coffee and set the cup on the floor. She snuggled up and rested her head on Michael's chest. "So what do you say?"

Michael stroked her hair. "Will you apologize to Emily?"

"No," Paris said promptly. "Want to go anyway?"

For a long moment Michael looked at her upside-down face on his chest. "Yes, I want to go anyway," he said at last, feeling half weary, half wonderful.

Dane walked up to Holly as she stood at the bathroom sink, dreamily brushing her hair. Judging by her expression, she was a million miles away. Dane wondered how long she would've stood there brushing if left to her own devices. Would she still have been there twelve hours later with a bald spot?

"Hello, Holly," he said lightly.

She jumped, then smiled at him in the mirror. "Hi, Dane."

Dane shifted from foot to foot. "So . . . it's all set for Saturday?"

"Hmm?" Holly said vaguely.

"Um, you remember—you know, *Saturday*," Dane said, suddenly feeling awkward.

Holly glanced at him, and then her eyes widened. "Oh, *that*. Sure, it's all set. I asked Emily if she wanted to go see *Casablanca*. I'll pretend to get stuck on campus, and she'll be here waiting for me."

He watched Holly, who was still brushing the same section of hair. The sight reminded Dane of the extremely poor quality of his sister's back rubs, the way she got distracted and scratched the same square inch of his back until it felt as if she was scraping exposed nerve. "Maybe you could say you lost track of time," he suggested ironically.

"Hey, that's a good idea," Holly said earnestly. "I do lose track of time sometimes."

"Really? You do?" Dane said, trying hard not to smile.

She looked at him in the mirror. "You really like Emily, don't you?"

Dane leaned against the doorjamb. "It's amazing. I like her more than my kindergarten teacher, Miss Finney, who used to make me stand in the corner. I like her—"

But just then the phone rang, and Holly jackrabbited past him faster than Dane had thought possible.

Holly scampered lightly across the landing to the pay phone. The pay phone was Holly's favorite feature of the house. To her, it was like having a jukebox or a video game machine all your own. Sometimes she even put quarters in it, although it wasn't necessary.

She picked up the heavy receiver. "Hello?" she said, hoping she didn't sound breathless.

"Holly?" said a deep voice. "It's—it's me."

Holly practically shivered with pleasure. It was

Mr. O'Halloran. And he'd said *It's me*. She had picked up the telephone, and the very man she'd been daydreaming about had said *It's me*. Holly felt the world of dating and love and relationships open wide to welcome her in.

"It's Alan," Mr. O'Halloran said hesitantly, evidently mistaking Holly's enthusiastic pause for confusion.

"Oh, I know," Holly said. She was thinking how completely wonderful this moment was when she realized he'd said something.

"I'm sorry I couldn't call you before this," Mr. O'Halloran said. "But I'm out of town."

"Really?" Holly said. "Where did you go?"

"Oh, just to the mountains," Mr. O'Halloran said evasively. "Listen . . . I'm not going to be back until Monday. Can I call you then?"

"Sure," Holly said, disappointed that she wouldn't see him sooner. "You can call me Monday."

"Okay," Mr. O'Halloran said. "We'll work out your schedule at the gallery and everything."

"Okay."

There was a pause, then Mr. O'Halloran began laughing.

"What?" Holly said. "What are you laughing about?"

Mr. O'Halloran sighed. "I'm laughing because I wanted to call you and say that I can't stop thinking about you and how much I wanted to kiss you the other night, and instead I started talking about work schedules— Oh, damn, I have to go. I'll talk to you on Monday, right?"

"Oh, yes," Holly breathed. Mr. O'Halloran had wanted to kiss her! "Oh, yes, Alan," she said again.

She hung up the receiver and leaned dreamily against the wall next to the pay phone. *That was the greatest phone call of my life,* she thought.

The pay phone made a clunking noise and, like a good omen, a quarter came zooming out of the coin return. Holly caught it with her left hand and walked away, whistling.

Chapter 12

THAT NIGHT MAC WAS LATE TO dinner, which pleased Dane—this was his chance to sit next to Emily. But Emily had cooked dinner, and she was too nervous and busy hopping up to get the roasted chicken and the baked potatoes, and then the gravy, and then more rolls, that Dane didn't have a chance to tell her about the time his sister had tried to make baked potatoes in the microwave, only she wrapped them in tinfoil first and almost blew the house up.

It turned out that the reason Mac was late was because he'd been listening to the weather report. "I'm going kayaking this weekend," he announced to the table. "Does anyone want to go with me?"

"Kayaking?" Michael repeated. "Won't you freeze to death?"

"I'll wear a wet suit," Mac explained. "So? Any takers?"

"I have to go visit my aunt in Colorado Springs," Paris replied, sounding regretful. "Believe me, I'd rather go kayaking."

Michael cleared his throat. "I'm going on a premed retreat," he said casually. "Otherwise I'd love to."

Emily paused, her fork halfway to her mouth. "I didn't know you were going on a retreat."

"Neither did I," Michael responded lightly. "They only left a message about it in my mailbox this morning."

Mac looked around the table. Holly shook her head, and Emily said she had to study.

"Dane?"

"Rehearsal," he said, secretly thrilled. So everyone was going to be away. His dinner with Emily was bound to work out. "And as long as we're making house invitations, my band is playing at The Bottleneck tonight if anyone wants to come."

"Hey, that would be great," Mac said. "I'm not leaving until the morning, anyway." He looked at Holly. "What do you say?"

"Okay," Holly said softly. She looked at Emily. "You want to come with us?"

Emily glanced at Holly and shrugged. "Sure," she said, avoiding Dane's eyes.

"Well, let's all go," Michael said. "We've never done anything as a group."

He glanced at Paris, who, Dane thought, looked a little uncomfortable, but she nodded.

"It's all set, then," Dane announced, taking a bite of his roll. He could hardly contain himself. He was going to see Emily two nights in a row (even if she wasn't aware of his plans for Saturday night yet). The thought of this made him so happy that he told story after story about people such as the high school music teacher who used to scratch herself with her baton, until even Emily smiled.

The five housemates lined up at the bar of The Bottleneck, listening to Dane's band and feeling, respectively, bored, thoughtful, conspicuous, thrilled, confused, and happy.

Paris was bored. Her jaw had almost dropped open when Michael had said the whole house should go out that night. She had been thinking that she and Michael could be alone if everyone else went. She wondered if he was trying to show Emily that he was willing to act like a member of one big, happy family. She sighed impatiently and tried to concentrate on the music. Dane had a surprisingly sexy voice, she thought impersonally. She moved closer to Michael and brushed her hand against his leg. He smiled at her, his beautiful blue eyes sparkling.

Mac was thoughtful, his mind turned toward his kayaking trip the next day. He was already mentally paddling down the river.

Emily felt conspicuous. Bars were not really her scene. She couldn't understand what all the fuss was about, though she supposed Dane's band was good. At first she had feared that Dane would dedicate a song to her. But so far he had dedicated songs to girls named Trish, Monica, Sara, and Delilah instead. And the song dedicated to Delilah had even been called "Delilah's Smile." Emily looked around the audience covertly, trying

to figure out who Delilah was. She guessed it was
a beautiful girl with shaggy dark hair standing
near the stage. Well, so maybe he wasn't going to
dedicate a song to Emily. *Which, of course, is
something I can be grateful for,* she told herself.
She looked around the bar. Maybe she would
meet some nice guy there that night. It would
serve Dane right. But all she saw were female
faces—young, pretty, and staring at Dane.

Holly was thrilled. Mr. O'Halloran had called
her. He would call again on Monday! These two
sentences beat steadily in her head, and she
dreamily adjusted the rhythm to whatever song
the band was playing. What would he say on
Monday? Oh, he would have to ask to see her
again! Someone was touching Holly's arm. It was
Emily. "Come on," she said. "We're going home."

Holly looked around, confused. "Shouldn't we
wait for Dane's band to play?" she asked. Emily
smiled and squeezed her hand.

Michael was happy because they didn't ask for
ID at The Bottleneck. He'd brought thirty dollars
with him and he spent all of it. The Bottleneck had
lots of imported beers, and Michael was trying to
drink one from every country. He'd had nine—one
each from Canada, England, Germany, Ireland,
Japan, Mexico, Portugal, Yugoslavia, and the
United States—when suddenly it was time to go.

"Come *on.*" Paris was tugging at his arm.
"Everyone's waiting for us."

"Okay," Michael said thickly. "Okay. All right.
Good. Fine."

"Just come on," Paris said.

They trailed out into the parking lot, and everyone squashed into Mac's car. Michael was in the back between Paris and Emily. Mac began backing the car out.

"Wait!" Michael shouted.

Mac slammed on the brakes so hard the car bounced. "What?"

"Not so fast," Michael said, trying to speak clearly. "Don't drive so fast."

"I was going five miles an hour," Mac protested. He began backing out again.

"Slower," Michael objected slackly. "And don't turn any corners."

Emily glanced at him. "Michael," she said, "how are we going to get home if we don't go around any corners?"

He shrugged and rested his head against her shoulder. "I don't know, Emmy," he said. "But I don't feel very good when he goes around corners."

Emily frowned and pushed his head off her shoulder. He slumped the other way, onto Paris, who let him stay there.

Dane had to tell the man behind the counter of the gourmet shop the whole story. Of course, being Dane, he didn't make it a very *short* story. In fact, it took him over ten minutes.

The man behind the counter was leaning on an elbow, looking sleepy. "So, what is it you want?" he asked.

"I want to marry her," Dane said, entranced. "I want to—"

"No," the man said patiently. "What do you want from me?"

"Oh," Dane said. "Well, I'm cooking her dinner. I thought I said that. Anyway, it has to be, like, the best dinner ever."

The man sighed. His name was Mr. Kaminsky, and he was not a romantic at heart. "Okay," he said wearily. "Let's see what we can do."

Half an hour later, Mr. Kaminsky was ringing up Dane's purchases. "Hey, that's a lot of money," Dane remarked as he paid. "Do I get a refund if she doesn't like it?"

"Sorry," Mr. Kaminsky said. "But if I were you, I'd buy some flowers. And candles."

"Hey, that's a good idea!" Dane said enthusiastically, as though Mr. Kaminsky had suggested something completely original.

"Well, you'll need all the help you can get," said Mr. Kaminsky, who had four daughters and was privately hoping that none of them ever hooked up with the likes of this guy with the dirty red bandanna. He would have been horrified to learn that his daughter Trish had had a song dedicated to her by Dane himself the night before.

Emily met Michael coming up the stairs as she was going down to the kitchen. He had an entire carton of orange juice in his hand.

"Well," she said, gesturing to the carton, "I guess I don't need to ask how you're feeling."

"It's just a hangover," Michael said uneasily. "Don't make a big deal out of it."

Emily raised an eyebrow. "I didn't realize I was making a big deal out of it," she said.

"Em . . ."

"Of course," she continued, "some people might think that asking the driver not to move forward or turn corners was a big deal. Some people might think tripping and banging your head against the kitchen table was a big deal. Some people might think that falling asleep—or should I say passing out?—with a spoonful of spaghetti sauce still in your mouth was a big—"

"Give it a rest," snapped Michael, whose mouth still tasted of tomatoes and onions. He was interested in what she'd said about the fall in the kitchen; that explained the bruise on his chin.

He looked at his sister with resentment. She was wearing gray sweats and a pale yellow sweatshirt. She looked amazingly rested and fresh and pretty.

"Don't take your hangover out on me," she said coldly.

"Then stop treating it like a federal offense," Michael said. "It was just a night out."

Emily shook her head. "You're not fooling me, Michael," she said. "I know you drink, and I know how much you drink. I remember what it was like when Dad drank, you know."

Michael's breath caught in his lungs. He glanced at Emily, but her eyes were merely angry, not knowing.

She doesn't really know, he thought. *She may suspect something, but she doesn't really have any idea.*

"I remember, too," he said. "But I'm not like that."

She slipped past him on the staircase. "I won't keep you," she said sarcastically. "I know you have to get ready for your *retreat.*"

He turned around. "What does that mean?"

"It means that I know you have to get ready for your retreat," Emily said carefully. "You wouldn't want to keep Paris waiting."

"Paris?"

"Yes, Paris," Emily said. "Isn't that another word for premed retreat?"

"What are you talking about?"

He had never seen her look so angry. "You and Paris, you idiot," she said. "Did you honestly think I didn't know?"

"I think you're projecting," Michael said. He was dizzy and his head hurt. He felt as though it might roll off his shoulders and smash like a pumpkin. "When you're not running up to the attic to flirt with Mac, you're running down to the basement to flirt with Dane."

But Emily was no longer listening. She had turned her back and was halfway down the stairs, running her hand lightly along the banister as though he weren't there and speaking to her, as though he weren't her brother, as though she had, finally, had enough of him.

Chapter 13

BY FIVE O'CLOCK, DANE WAS exhausted and the kitchen looked as though someone had fought hard for his life, hurling every pot, pan, and utensil at an intruder. Greasy spoons clung to the counters, food-encrusted pots and pans towered in the sink. The floor was spattered with food stains and Dane's sticky footprints.

But Dane was pleased. He had made acorn-squash soup; wine-braised quail with sage, leeks, and shiitake mushrooms; kasha pilaf; and baked apples with macaroon soufflé for dessert. Originally he had planned an artichoke salad, too, but his hands were so cramped and covered with little cuts that he decided to skip it.

Now Dane checked everything one last time: the burners and oven were set on warm, the soufflé batter was sitting in a bowl waiting for the egg whites. Everything would be okay on its own for a few minutes.

He scampered downstairs and showered in his

dingy shower. Then he sneaked upstairs in a towel and went through Michael's closet. It was just as he suspected: boring banker clothes. Still, maybe that was what Emily would like. Dane was shorter than Michael, so Michael's pants wouldn't work, but he took a white shirt and green tie, plus a pair of green socks, and went back to his room to dress.

He combed his light brown hair back and bounced up the stairs. He had just finished setting the table—flowers! candles! thank you, Mr. Kaminsky!—when Emily came down the stairs with her purse in her hand.

"Has Holly come back yet?" she asked him. "We're supposed to go to a movie and she's really late." She paused, looking at him carefully. "Why are you staring at me?"

"Because—" Dane swallowed. "I wanted to make you dinner. I mean, I did make you dinner. I was afraid if I asked, you'd say no, so I—I just did."

He picked up one of the cloth napkins on the table and began twisting it.

Emily looked at him for a long time. She glanced at the table, and her eyes took in the flowers and candles.

"You made dinner for me?" she asked gently.

Dane nodded. "A-And, um, Holly just called," he stammered. "She said she's—stuck on campus."

"I see." The faintest smile flickered across her lips. Then she slid her purse off her shoulder and sat down at the table. "This looks lovely," she said softly. "Shall we start?"

Michael slept in the passenger seat while Paris drove the three hours to Estes Park. When he woke, he felt much better, although he could *still* taste spaghetti sauce.

"Tell me again," he said to Paris as she parked the car. "Why did I want to have spaghetti in the middle of the night?"

"Don't ask *me*," Paris said. "But you were totally insistent, and then while I was heating the sauce, you scooped up a big mouthful and passed out before you could swallow it. You really don't remember?"

Michael shook his head. "Wasn't anybody worried that I would choke to death?"

Paris rolled her eyes. "We were all relieved when you conked out and quit blathering incoherently." She smiled. "Everyone except for me, of course," she said wryly. "I find you fascinating all the time."

"Thanks, sweetie." Michael touched the ends of her hair.

She kissed him. "Come on, let's go inside."

They got out of the car and went into Paris's father's condo. Michael walked through it, amazed. It had five bedrooms, three baths, two fireplaces, a living room, a dining room, and a kitchen.

"Jeez, this place is bigger than the house on Spruce Street," he marveled. "And about a million times nicer."

"Well, that's my father for you," Paris said, walking past him. "He likes nice things."

Michael followed her, admiring the condominium: thick carpeting, elegant wallpaper, nubby chairs and couches, expensive art on the walls. "And this is just a ski place?" he asked.

"Yeah," Paris called from the kitchen. "Ridiculous, huh?"

He came into the kitchen. She was poking around in the refrigerator. "Hmm," she said. "We're going to have to live all weekend on a potato, it seems."

Michael was staring at the far wall of the kitchen. He licked his lips without realizing it. "What about that?" he asked, pointing to the liquor cabinet.

Paris looked. "What about it?"

"Can we—can we drink some?"

"Sure." Paris shrugged. "Go ahead."

"Won't your father notice?"

"No, he'll think it's my stepmother. She likes to drink almost as much as you do."

Michael glanced at her. "Meaning?"

"Nothing," Paris said breezily. "You can polish off every bottle if you want to. I don't care if my father knows or not."

Michael was already opening the doors of the cabinet. After he poured himself a Scotch, he held up a glass for her, but she shook her head. "Your father doesn't care if you drink?"

She shrugged. "Minding your own business is a big deal in my family."

"Oh," Michael said absently. The Scotch was working its usual magic. "Come here, beautiful," he said to Paris.

"This is so elegant," Emily said softly as Dane served the soup. "I would have dressed up if you'd told me."

"You look great," Dane said sincerely. She was still wearing the pale yellow sweatshirt, and it made her creamy skin glow. The candlelight glinted on her glossy black hair. He sat down across from her.

Emily tasted her soup and smiled at him. "So, you never told me whether your sister got a nose job or not."

Dane grinned contentedly. "No, she didn't get it," he replied. "My dad drew the line at that, and my sister went back to the therapist and said, 'Look, he apparently just doesn't feel all that guilty.'"

"So that was the end of the nose job discussion?" Emily asked.

"Well, not really," Dane told her. "A couple of years later she took this pottery class, and she made all these bowls and vases and stuff, only they all had big ceramic noses."

Emily looked confused. "How can a bowl have a nose?"

"Yeah, well, exactly," Dane said. "I mean, you'd be eating a nice hot bowl of soup and suddenly you'd glimpse this *thing* at the bottom of the bowl, and you'd eat a little more soup, and you could see the thing more clearly now. And it was a nose."

"Why did she do that?"

"Because she said that was what her own nose felt like. Like she couldn't get away from it."

"Oh, the poor girl," Emily said. "And she never got her nose job?"

Dane shook his head. "Once she had all the money saved up for it, but then she saw a TV show about all these people whose nose jobs had gone hideously wrong, so she bought a Jeep instead." He brightened. "But the story has a happy ending after all, because the Jeep was recalled by the manufacturer and my sister took them to court."

"That's the happy ending?" Emily asked.

"Well, not *that* part of it," Dane said hastily. "She wound up marrying her lawyer."

"Oh," Emily said.

There was a moment of silence.

"Dane . . ." Emily toyed with her water glass. She looked at him. The candlelight darkened her blue eyes to the color of grape Popsicles. "I can't believe you did this for me," she said.

Dane felt his heart swell. "I—" he began, when suddenly the door burst open and the other four members of Pop Smear vaulted in as though shot from giant rubber bands.

Holly walked toward the arts building, feeling a little blue. She was happy to help Dane arrange his date with Emily, but it left her, Holly, at loose ends. Still, two more days and Mr. O'Halloran would be back. The thought lifted her spirits, and her steps quickened as she climbed the stairs of the deserted building.

In the sculpture room, she put on her blue

smock and tied her hair back in a ponytail. She unlocked her cupboard and regarded her first project critically. It was a bust of the boy who sat across from her in sculpture class. In the very first sculpture class Holly had ever taken, she had been too shy and inhibited to think up an original project, and she'd been so desperate that she finally just did a three-quarters-life-size bust of Tom Capella, the guy who sat across from her. She'd glazed it blue. Ever since then, she had made it a rule to do a bust of the person who sat across from her in sculpture class. She glazed them all in solid colors. She never even spoke to most of the people she chose as models, but the busts graced her room, five in all.

Her current sculpture looked all wrong to her. She thought maybe the forehead looked a little too Neanderthal. She was wondering how to correct that when there was a soft knock on the open door. "Holly?"

She looked up. Isabelle stood in the doorway. "Oh, hello," Holly said, genuinely pleased to see her.

"What are you doing here on a Saturday night?" Isabelle asked, coming into the room.

"Oh, I thought I'd do some work, but I'm really just daydreaming," Holly said. "What about you?"

"My husband's out of town, so I'm catching up on a few projects," Isabelle said. "Want to join me in the lounge for a cup of tea?"

"I'd love to," Holly said. She locked her project back up and followed Isabelle down the hall.

Isabelle poured them each a cup of hot water

from the ancient, stained coffeepot and dunked a tea bag in each cup. "Graciously served," she said, setting a cup in front of Holly. Holly smiled shyly as they settled down at the splintery lounge table.

"Listen," Isabelle said, taking a sip of tea, "I know I already said this, but your life drawing skills are really fantastic."

"Thanks," Holly said, blushing a little.

Isabelle looked at her for a moment. "Where have you studied, Holly?"

Holly shrugged. "Just classes at the Y and stuff like that," she said.

Isabelle smiled. "Well, you have tremendous natural talent."

"Thank you," Holly said again. "I think—I think life drawing is easy because I've spent so much time watching."

Isabelle frowned a little bit. "Watching what?"

Holly shifted uncomfortably in her chair. "People," she said.

Isabelle studied her for a moment, pursing her lips. "Watching from the outside, you mean?"

Holly nodded.

Isabelle looked thoughtful. "Well, it certainly shows in your work . . . but don't watch forever. Life is—well, it's too short for that." Suddenly she smiled and touched Holly's arm. "Sorry, I don't mean to lecture you."

"That's okay," Holly said. Actually, she liked it when people had firm opinions about life and how it should be lived. She wished people would advise her more often. In fact, when she was small, she had often imagined that there was a manual that explained how to live, step by step. It had been her fondest wish for years to read that manual and crack the code.

"Uh, guys . . . " Dane said, sending his friends warning looks.

"Hey, man, where have you *been?*" Lukie said. "Delilah is looking for you."

Dane saw Emily drop her eyes. "Guys, this is kind of a bad time," he began again, but they were swarming around Emily, introducing themselves—Lukie, Scorpio, K.O., and Seth. He watched as her small hand disappeared into their huge ones.

"Nice to meet you," she said, faintly flustered. "How are you?"

Seth took out a package of clove cigarettes. "Do you mind?" he said.

Emily shook her head, but Dane knew that she did mind. Seth lit his cigarette off one of the candles, extinguishing the candle in the process.

"Seth—" Dane began.

"Hey, Dane," Lukie boomed from the kitchen. "Something is seriously wrong with this chicken."

Dane looked through the doorway and saw that Lukie was eating directly from the pan with a barbecue fork.

Dane jumped to his feet. "Put that back!" he yelled, and ran into the kitchen. He grabbed the pan away from Lukie, but it was too late—the quail was pretty much mauled. "Lukie . . . "

"Hey, you should thank me," Lukie said. "I'm

telling you, that chicken was past its prime or something."

"It wasn't chicken, it was quail," Dane moaned. He grabbed Lukie by the collar. "Now take the others and get out of here," he said hoarsely.

They went back into the dining room to find that K.O. was braiding the centerpiece flowers into Seth's hair. He glanced up and saw Dane's angry look.

"Hey," he said, "I started to do her hair"—he gestured to Emily—"but she wouldn't let me."

"We're supposed to go," Lukie told the others, wiping his mouth with Emily's napkin. "They're, like, on a date or something."

"Date!" K.O. said. "You dog! What about Monica?"

"Yeah," Seth said. "Weren't you supposed to meet her tonight? Or did you meet her last night after the—"

"Get out!" Dane hollered, but Emily was already on her feet, the flower K.O. had started to weave into her hair still nestled behind her ear. She looked so beautiful that Dane thought he might start crying.

"There's no need for you to leave on my account," she said quietly. "We're finished here. All finished."

Paris and Michael sat in the Jacuzzi in the master bathroom, dizzy with heat. They were drinking a bottle of wine from Paris's father's liquor cabinet, or rather, Michael was drinking it. Paris said she never wanted to feel hung over again.

Michael looked at Paris fondly. Her blond hair was water-dark, slicked back from her face. He admired the perfection of her features, the delicate arch of her silky eyebrows.

Paris saw him looking and smiled. "Hey," she said. "I'm about to pass out."

"Just a few more minutes," Michael said, reaching for her. He pulled her close to him in the bubbling water. "This is nice," he said. "Just the two of us." He took a sip of wine. "This place is amazing. Why *do* you live at Spruce Street, by the way?" he asked. "You could live anywhere and avoid all the hassle."

"Is *hassle* another word for Emily?" Paris asked, laughing.

"Maybe." Michael grinned sheepishly. "But you haven't answered my question. I mean, your dad would pay for you to have your own place, right?"

Paris looked at him for a long time. "Let me tell you a secret," she said. "My dad thinks he *is* paying for an apartment in Boulder."

"He does?"

She nodded, smiling. "He sends me seven hundred and fifty dollars a month for rent."

"No way!" Michael exclaimed. "That's a lot of money."

She shrugged. "He can afford it."

"Still—" Michael began.

"Oh, don't go all soft and moralistic on me," Paris broke in, splashing him with water. "What's the big deal? I just like the idea of pulling something over on him. And money is his favorite thing by far."

"You don't like him very much, do you?"

"Well, aren't *you* perceptive," Paris said sarcastically. "No, I don't like him very much at all."

"Why?"

"*Why?*" Paris repeated. "For the same reason you don't like hard-boiled eggs."

"I do like hard-boiled eggs."

"That was just an example. Do you like lima beans?"

"Don't change the subject, Paris," Michael said. "Look, sweetie, I trust you. If you don't like your father, I'm sure there's a very good reason. I just wondered what it was."

"There are plenty of reasons," Paris said, sitting up straighter and splashing him again in the process. "I hate him because—because—"

"Just tell me," Michael said gently.

Paris sighed. "Okay," she said. "You know that night I said that I was named Paris because that's where I was conceived?"

Michael nodded.

Paris looked far into the distance, her face tightening. "Well, that wasn't the truth."

"No?" Michael asked when Paris fell silent.

"No." Paris turned to him, her face still hard and her eyes blazing. "I'm named after my father's mistress. *She* was conceived in Paris, and *her* parents named her that, and she just happened to be the girl my father was screwing when my mother had me! And he thought she had a pretty name—" Her voice cracked.

"Hey, hey." Stunned, Michael gathered her into his arms. "Oh, Paris."

He held her very close, burying his face in her hair and rubbing small circles on her back, not saying anything, because truly, he could think of nothing to say.

Midnight found Emily and Holly perched on the wrought-iron bench on the roof, eating a big bowl of chocolate-chip cookie dough with the same spoon. Such are the joys of close friendship.

Holly licked the spoon. "I still don't see why you're so angry with him. It sounds lovely."

"It was humiliating," Emily said, taking the spoon and digging into the bowl. "When his friends showed up and started talking about those other girls, I realized that he was only pretending to be sweet. He's not really like that."

"But how do you know that's his real self?" Holly asked. "Maybe the sweet self is the real one."

"Well, one of the selves took off in the van and hasn't come back yet," Emily said. "Want to bet where he is? And anyway"—she poked Holly in the arm with the sticky spoon—"don't go defending him. I'm mad at you, too. How could you agree to set me up like that?"

Holly sighed. "I'm sorry. I guess I'm just a sucker for romance."

"Hey, speaking of that, how's Mr. O'Halloran?"

Holly beamed. "He comes back on Monday and then he's going to call me."

Emily looked skeptical. "I hope you know what you're doing."

Holly's face clouded.

"I'm sorry, sugarplum," Emily said hastily. "I shouldn't interfere."

"That's okay," Holly said softly. "But I do know what I'm doing."

They finished the rest of the ice cream in silence, watching the empty street for Dane's van, which didn't appear.

Chapter 14

THE NEXT MORNING, MICHAEL woke up with a hangover that would have pained even a heavy drinker and probably paralyzed a light one. But Michael was drinking so much these days that his hangover only registered as a low-grade headache.

Paris, who was already up and packing, tossed a T-shirt to him. "Come on, it's late," she said.

Michael sat up groggily and pulled on the T-shirt. Paris went into the bathroom.

"Paris?" he called.

"Hmm?" She came back with a jumble of cosmetics in her arms. She dumped them into her overnight bag.

"Paris." Michael tried to catch her arm, but she was too far away. "Paris, if you want to talk about your father—"

"I don't want to talk about my father."

"Well, last night you—"

Paris flashed him a brittle smile. "I think I said I didn't want to talk about my father," she said, moving from dresser to overnight bag and back again.

Dane and Emily shared an uncomfortable brunch of Pop-Tarts, chocolate with chocolate frosting.

Emily toyed with her Pop-Tart and wondered where Dane had gone the previous night. Monica's? Delilah's? Or maybe he'd been with someone else altogether. Why did she care anyway? Had she actually considered joining his harem? She must've been crazy.

Dane was scraping the frosting off his Pop-Tart with his teeth, enjoying the way it broke into pieces like paint flakes. He was thinking about a game he and his sister had made up about six years ago. The game was called If Mom Were Being Held Hostage, With Whom Would You Be Willing to Spend a Night of Passion in Order to Save Her Life?

Dane and his sister had amused themselves through countless car rides with this game, until one day his sister said, "Look, you're never going to find someone so revolting that I wouldn't spend a night of passion with them in order to save Mom. This game is just a way of grossing ourselves out," and they'd lost interest in playing. But now Dane was considering asking Emily to play the game. He wanted to know if she'd be willing to spend a night of passion with *him* in order to save her mother. He thought she probably wouldn't. He thought she would probably let her mother perish.

Emily turned to him abruptly. "*Must* you scrape the frosting off with your teeth?" she said irritably. "It makes the most disgusting noise."

Before he could respond, Holly came down from upstairs, and Paris, Michael, and Mac burst through the kitchen door. The six of them exchanged grateful looks, perhaps not especially happy to see each other, but very happy not to be alone with their thoughts anymore.

Dane made macaroni and cheese for dinner and served it to five very quiet people. They seemed to be hungry people, though, because they attacked their food ravenously. There was no sound but their chewing.

"So," Michael said finally. "Did anything exciting happen this weekend?"

"No!" Emily and Dane said together, quickly and nervously.

There was another silence.

"Actually," Dane said, "I did have an interesting thought this weekend."

Emily looked up apprehensively. "You did?"

"I think we should have a party Monday night," Dane said.

Emily raised an eyebrow. "Why's that?"

"I just think having a party on Monday is a good idea," Dane explained. "No one ever throws parties on Monday."

"Dane," Emily said, "no one ever throws parties on Monday because it's the very beginning of the week, and people have classes on Tuesday."

"Yes, but only hopelessly neurotic people think about those classes on Monday night," Dane said. His green eyes glinted at her. "People would much rather go to a party if only there was a party to go to."

"I think a party sounds like fun," Michael said.

"But tomorrow night?" Paris said. "That's so soon."

"Well, there are six of us," Mac said. "If we each invite ten people, we could fill the house."

Dane looked happy. "The guys and I can set up in a corner," he said.

"I don't think I know ten people," Holly said anxiously.

"That's okay," Emily said, standing up and beginning to clear the table. "I'm sure Dane will invite at least fifty hopeful girls."

Emily and Mac did the dishes that night, which was actually a pretty easy job because Dane had been so hungry that he'd attacked the macaroni pan with a fork and scraped out every morsel. Emily barely had to do more than rinse it.

"So," Mac said, taking the pan from her, "how did your dinner with Dane go?"

Emily rolled her eyes. "Jeez, how fast does word travel around here?"

Mac laughed. "About the speed of light, I guess. The other day I went to see a movie, and Paris saw the ticket stub in the trash and asked me about a million times who I saw it with."

Emily was curious despite herself. "Well . . . who did you see it with?"

Mac smiled. "By myself."

"Oh." Emily blushed. "I'm sorry. I didn't mean to pry."

"That's okay," Mac said. "I don't think people should have secrets."

"I think people need a few secrets," Emily said hesitantly. She began washing the silverware. "It keeps them whole."

Mac shook his head. "Secrets are nothing but trouble." He took a handful of knives from her and began rinsing them.

"But you—" Emily said, and then paused.

"But I what?" Mac's voice was gently puzzled.

Emily scrubbed a fork miserably. Now she sounded like a gossip. "Well, it's just that Holly said you went to Exeter."

"I did go to Exeter," Mac said softly. "That's not a secret. If you're interested, all you had to do was ask."

"But if you went to Exeter, why aren't you at Harvard?" Emily blurted out. "Or wherever?"

For a long moment Mac rinsed the forks in silence. "I went to Exeter," he said finally. "But I didn't graduate from there. I was expelled."

"Oh," Emily said, biting her lip. "What—what did— I mean, why?"

Mac smiled faintly. "You mean, what did I do?"

She nodded.

He sighed again. "Exeter has an honor code," he said softly. "I saw a guy cheating on a Latin test and I didn't turn him in. The teacher saw him cheating and me *seeing* him cheating, and we were both expelled."

"That's awful," Emily gasped. "That's the most

unfair thing I ever heard of. Surely your parents could have appealed, or—or—"

"Oh, they appealed," Mac said easily. "But Exeter's honor code is written in stone. Besides, my dad agreed with the school."

"Are you kidding?" Emily stared at Mac. "He couldn't have!"

Mac shrugged. "You don't know my dad. He went to Exeter. His father did. His father's father did. And *his* father was in the first class to graduate from the place." He laughed softly. "My family probably has more money than Paris's. That's another secret for you."

Emily realized her hands had been in the steaming dishwater for several minutes. She pulled them out. They were pink and raw-looking. "Is your father still angry?"

Mac shook his head. "He was never angry," he said. "He said that I did what I thought was right. But we used to be close and now we're not. We—we don't talk on the phone, and I've only seen them twice since it happened."

Emily stared at her hands, trying to imagine what it would be like if she couldn't call her family. Of course, every time she did call, her mother said, *Dear, I saw Frank's mother at the supermarket and she said that Frank is in the top five percent of his class!* and then her father got on the phone and said, *Are you studying hard? Good, then let's cut this short, it's costing a fortune.* It was maddening. But she could still call them. They were still her parents.

A tear slipped down Emily's cheek, hotter than the dishwater.

"Oh, Em," Mac said softly. "Don't do that." He wiped her face with his hands, which were dripping wet.

"You're getting my face wetter than it *was*," Emily said, but she smiled a little.

Mac said nothing, still rubbing at her face gently with his fingers. Then he leaned forward and kissed her.

It was a long, slow kiss, and Emily thought fleetingly that maybe if her hands weren't covered with suds she would have put them around his neck. Instead she pulled away and said hoarsely, "Please don't do that again."

Then she walked away, very slowly and with some poise. Not until she reached her room did she start shaking.

Chapter 15

EVERYTHING OF INTEREST THAT
was to happen at the party happened in either the
kitchen or the bathroom. This is the way of most
parties, and maybe someday people will realize
this and plan accordingly, but such was not the
case at the house on Spruce Street.

Holly vacuumed the threadbare living room rug
and dusted the ancient curlicues of the scratched
furniture. Dane and his band set up in the corner,
where they rehearsed loudly and happily all afternoon. Emily and Mac festooned the walls with gar-
lands of crepe paper and bouquets of balloons.
(This took them somewhat longer than it might
have, considering how careful they were not to let
their fingers touch when they handed each other
the scissors or the masking tape.) Michael made
the punch in the kitchen. He had planned to spike
it, but then Emily made him chop up around eight
hundred carrots, so he drank the bottle of rum
himself to break the monotony. Paris wandered
around languidly in her green silk robe with her

hair rolled around orange-juice cans and her fingernail polish drying.

The first guest arrived at quarter to eight, while they were all in their respective rooms, changing. By the time they were all finished and downstairs, over seventy-five people were crowding the already sagging floors of the house.

Since Paris was the last one ready (her hair took some arranging, though it now fell in graceful waves over her shoulders, thanks to the orange-juice cans) she was the only one who heard the phone ring. It was already too noisy downstairs. She answered the pay phone on the second landing.

"Oh, hello, Mr. O'Halloran," she said. She listened for a moment. "Well, we're having a party here. Can I give her a message?" She listened again. "Okay . . . Yeah, I'll tell her. . . . Thanks."

Paris hung up the phone. She stood still for a moment, readjusting her sleeveless blue dress and finger-combing her hair. Then she went downstairs to give Holly the message.

Michael and Emily met in the kitchen at eight-thirty.

"Look at this," Michael said indignantly. "I spent about five hours chopping vegetables, and those *animals* devoured them in fifteen minutes."

Emily shrugged and reached into the freezer for another bag of ice. "Well, that's what happens at parties." She was wearing a red velvet dress and gold hoop earrings. Her dark hair was caught in a gold clasp at the nape of her neck.

"Emily . . . " Michael said. He waited until she looked up at him. "Can't we be friends again?"

She raised an eyebrow. "Am I being unfriendly?"

"You know you are."

"I'm sorry." She smiled. "I wasn't aware of it. I'll try to be more polite." She turned to go.

"I'm not talking about polite!" Michael said. He caught her arm. "You're my sister, Em. Can't we rely on each other to—to—"

"To be honest and tell the truth?" Emily said. "My point exactly."

She freed her arm from his grasp impersonally, as though he were nothing more to her than an overeager dance partner, and left the room.

Holly was listening to some guy prattle on about his linguistics class and thinking that she didn't like parties because she always got stuck talking to people like this guy.

She was also thinking that she shouldn't have worn her cream-colored suit because somebody was bound to spill something on it.

Paris tapped her on the shoulder. "Mr. O'Halloran called for you," she said. "He wants you to meet him at the gallery."

Holly beamed. "Thank you, Paris," she said, sounding as though Paris had just saved her life. Without so much as saying good-bye to the boring guy, she bounced out the door.

Michael was drinking Scotch and milk out of his bathroom thermos when a loud banging on the door nearly made him choke.

"Listen, whoever you are!" Paris shouted. "This bathroom is strictly off limits! If the line downstairs is long, that's too bad!"

He opened the door. "It's me."

"Oh," Paris said. "Well, hello, you."

He smiled and pulled her inside with him, cornering her against the sink. He kissed the side of her neck. "So what's going on downstairs?"

"Not much," Paris said ruefully, running her hands up his back. "There are about a hundred girls throwing their underpants at the band. Emily is talking to her Environmental Law professor while he looks down her dress."

"So we're not missing anything?" Michael said. He kissed the tip of her nose.

Paris shook her head.

"Then let's get out of here," Michael said. "Let's go back up to Estes Park."

"Okay," Paris said. She curled an arm around his neck and kissed him. "Whatever you say."

They slipped down the stairs and out the front door, where their breath made white plumes as fluffy as cotton.

Dane was in the kitchen, eating peanut butter from a jar with a fork, when Emily came in.

"Hey, how come you're not out there with the band?" she asked.

He shrugged. "I don't want to sing the whole time. Plus I needed some energy." He licked the fork, then washed it at the sink, holding it up to the light when he was through.

Emily laughed. "So *you're* the person who made the clean-tines rule," she said. "I always wondered."

Dane looked surprised for a moment, then nodded. "I hate it when there's gunk between the tines," he said. He dried his hands on a dish towel and then stood next to her by the refrigerator, reading the house rules.

"I think Mac wrote the fingernail clippings rule," he said. "I saw him clipping his toenails over a paper bag once."

"Well, I know that Holly wrote the one about channel surfing," Emily said. "Because her father does that all the time. And Michael's probably the only one hyper enough to write that thing about more than one but less than three ice cubes."

"You know," Dane said thoughtfully, "I'll bet everyone thinks I wrote the one about not singing if you can't carry a tune."

"Oh, no, I wrote that *about* you," Emily said. "I was afraid you'd sing all the time and not have a nice voice."

He looked at her.

"But you do have a nice voice," she said awkwardly.

He smiled. "Do you realize what just happened?"

"I think I just insulted you," Emily said uncertainly.

"No," Dane said impatiently. "We just had a

conversation that didn't end with your storming out of the room."

He reached up and brushed a stray hair off her face. Emily realized that she was standing closer to Dane than she ever had before, and she couldn't think of anything to say. He smelled nice, like cinnamon and matches and toothpaste. They were deceptive smells, she knew, these nice homey smells that made you think you were with someone kind and familiar.

Dane's eyes were only inches from hers, bright and green and watchful.

He's going to kiss me, Emily thought, panicked. *Unless I do something, he's going to kiss me.*

She did nothing.

Main Street was dark as a cave when Holly reached the gallery, but the Open sign hung in the window, and the door was unlocked when she tried it. She stepped inside.

"Hello?" she called tentatively. There was no answer.

Holly was suddenly nervous that it had all been a joke. She knew a girl in high school who once got a phone call saying that she'd won free dance lessons, but when she showed up at the dance school, nobody had heard of her, and it was embarrassing beyond words.

"Holly?"

She jumped and turned around. It was Mr. O'Halloran. He stood next to her in the darkened gallery.

"Sorry I scared you."

"That's okay," Holly said, swallowing hard. "You wanted to see me?"

"Yes," Mr. O'Halloran said, then fell silent.

Holly wondered how long they were going to stand here like this. Should she suggest they move to the back room and talk? To the supply room?

She could hear Mr. O'Halloran's breathing, and suddenly she wanted to feel his heart beating. Almost of its own volition her hand crept out and laid itself flat against his chest. Yes, she could feel his heart, booming softly, as though from a great distance.

"Oh, Holly," he said. He moved closer to her and ran his fingers along her collarbone. "Oh, Holly."

He's going to kiss me! Holly thought delightedly. *He's going to kiss me, and I didn't even have to maneuver him into the supply room!*

Mr. O'Halloran's fingers slipped upward from her collarbone until he cupped her face. He kissed her gently.

Holly felt something like happiness rising through her like a balloon, until she was almost sure she could feel it attached to the top of her head, tugging gently.

Mac watched with impersonal fascination as his supervisor from Sports City, Lorraine, threw underwear at various members of Dane's band. This was perhaps not so sordid as it sounds, since Lorraine took the underwear out of her purse and not off her body. Mac wondered if she'd brought them to the party for just such a purpose or what.

He watched as Carolyn from ski wear tried to apply her lipstick, using the toaster on the dining room table as a mirror.

The assistant manager, Rob, was inhaling furiously on an unlit cigarette.

Suddenly, and for no particular reason, Mac wondered what was keeping Emily in the kitchen. He set down his glass of punch and went to find her.

Michael had brought his thermos with him, and he held it between his legs as he drove Paris's BMW.

Paris watched him critically. "Are you sure you're okay to drive?" she asked. "Because I can take over."

"I'm sure," Michael said. He lifted the thermos and drank the last few swallows. "There," he said, handing the thermos to her. "I'm all through."

"That's what worries me," Paris murmured. She took the thermos and put it on the floor.

She decided to let him drive till the halfway point and then tell him she'd take over. *He seems alert enough,* she told herself. Besides, she was so sleepy, and she wanted to relax for a little while.

The halfway point was five miles away. Paris leaned her head back against the seat and closed her eyes.

And because her eyes were closed, she didn't see the curve in the road. Michael didn't see it because he was drunk and thought the road was straight. Consequently they were both quite calm and there were no last-minute cries or swerves or screeching of tires—the BMW simply sailed straight off the road at seventy-two miles per hour.

Its flight was beautiful in a way, a gentle curving arc. Witnesses, had there been any, might have admired the way the BMW seemed to hang in midair for a moment before it began falling down the embankment, faster than the speed of light.

At that moment Dane kissed Emily, and it seemed to her that all the furniture in the kitchen, including the refrigerator, rose about six inches off the ground.

She had the distinct impression that if she continued kissing him, the furniture and appliances would begin swirling around them, faster and faster, until they broke free of the kitchen, perhaps free of the house, and walls would burst open, ceilings would cave in, the furnace would explode.

She slipped her arms around Dane's neck. Mind you, she has always been a sentimental fool.

🏠 HarperPaperbacks *By Mail*

They'd all grown up together on a tiny island. They thought they knew everything about one another. . . . But they're only just beginning to find out the truth.

BOYFRIENDS GIRLFRIENDS

#1 Zoey Fools Around

#2 Jake Finds Out

#3 Nina Won't Tell

#4 Ben's In Love

#5 Claire Gets Caught

#6 What Zoey Saw

#7 Lucas Gets Hurt

#8 Aisha Goes Wild

And don't miss these bestselling *Ocean City* titles by Katherine Applegate:

#1 Ocean City

#2 Love Shack

#3 Fireworks

#4 Boardwalk

#5 Ocean City Reunion

#6 Heat Wave

#7 Bonfire

Look for these new titles in the *Freshman Dorm* series, also from HarperPaperbacks:

Super #6:
Freshman
Beach Party

Super #7:
Freshman
Spirit

Super #8:
Freshman
Noel